Three Dashes Bitters

Jack Simmons

swahorse

THREE DASHES BITTERS

A SwanHorse Press Book
Monte Ceceri Publishers, LLC

Cover photograph: Ed Eckstrand
New Orleans panorama: Kelly Sigga, FreeImages.com
Book design: Lisa Leppek

Special thanks to The Columns Hotel, The Bombay Club, Commander's Palace, and Antoine's Restaurant in New Orleans as well as Moon River Brewing Company, The Sentient Bean, *Connect Savannah*, and The Book Lady Bookstore in Savannah for their gracious support in this project.

First edition published by Palaver in 2017.

For additional information, special bulk, book club, and educational pricing, and other resources, please contact Monte Ceceri Publishers.

Publisher's Cataloguing-In-Publication Data:
Simmons, Jack, 1964– author
Three dashes bitters: A novel / Jack Simmons
ISBN: 978-1-949512-00-7 (paperback)
ISBN: 978-1-949512-01-4 (eBook)
1. Philosophy—Fiction. 2. Existentialism—Fiction. 3. New Orleans (La.)—Fiction. 4. Etiquette—Southern States—United States—Fiction. 5. American wit and humor. 6. Love stories, American. 7. United States—Fiction. I. Title

Monte Ceceri Publishers
P.O. Box 60623
Savannah, GA 31420
www.montececeri.com

In memory of
Sabrina Manganella Simmons

Contents

THREE DASHES BITTERS

The only thing to do with good advice is to pass it on.
It is never of any use to oneself.

Oscar Wilde

THE DATE

Most of the grounds of the world's
troubles are matters of grammar.

Montaigne

Sazerac

2 OZ RYE WHISKEY
3 DASHES PEYCHAUD'S BITTERS
1 TSP ABSINTHE
1 SUGAR CUBE
1 LEMON PEEL, TWISTED
Serve chilled, straight up, in a
rocks glass.

1

NOTHING UNNERVES LIKE A DATE with an ex-girlfriend. But this wasn't a date, and Jane wasn't an ex-girlfriend. She was just a friend, a female friend, whom I had slept with.

What was Jane? She wasn't my girlfriend, had never been my girlfriend. What do you call such a girl? What do you wear? A meeting with an old lover is like a barometer of your life. Look like a slob and she'll be relieved that it ended when it did. I didn't want her to be relieved. Jeans and a button-down? Or was this a blazer affair? It was definitely not an affair, just a meeting of two old friends to kick off my return to New Orleans.

I tried on all the shirts I had with me for my visit. That was, unfortunately, a total of three: a yellow polo, a white button-down, and a flannel. Three-week visit, three shirts, one suit, one tie. It wasn't going to be a *GQ* holiday. I chose the white button-down. I had packed more clothing, but the taxi driver left one of my suitcases on the curb at the airport, typical New Orleans efficiency. I called the airport for it in vain. That taxi driver was probably wearing my wool sport coat right now. I considered wearing the one suit I had brought, ash gray, European cut. It seemed a bit too much for having drinks at The Columns. I tried it on anyway.

It was years since I had seen her. We had only corresponded once during that time, an unfortunate exchange involving an ill-conceived Christmas card with reindeer. I had returned to New Orleans on more than one occasion, but this was the first time I had the guts to call her. Hell, I half-expected her to be married with kids. This expectation I knew to be false. Our families were close enough that I always heard news about her. But family news wasn't telling me what I wanted to know. I wasn't even sure what I wanted to know. I regretted not staying in touch with her, and I regretted calling her now. I regretted both.

The suit looked stupid, especially without a tie. I grabbed my one option and reflexively began the four-in-hand. My mother had given it to me for Christmas; of course, it was dreadful—a green and yellow pattern of golfers puzzled tightly together so as only to be distinguished from close inspection. I never quite understood the aesthetic. Who wears this stuff? Golfers? I guess it didn't matter what I wore. Jane was probably just trying not to be rude when she agreed to see me. She wasn't much for standing on tradition, but she was always polite. It was that combination that had always appealed to me. She had managed to dispense with the dreadfully proper attitude her parents had taught her without adopting the rebel-without-a-cause demeanor that was so common and tiresome.

I heard her horn. I guess she wasn't that polite. I ran wet fingers through my thinning brown hair, pulled the suit coat tightly around my narrow shoulders, and inspected my orthodontically corrected teeth for bits of a hasty dinner. My eyes wandered from my teeth to the rest of my face. I didn't look unattractive, although the jeans and button-down would have been the wiser choice. I recalled my mother having told my sisters, "A man's charm is defined by his character, not his looks." I am not sure they believed it, but I held out hope that some daughters did.

I snuck past my sister Tabatha's room where my mother, other sister Sarah, and Aunt Page were furiously taping and pinning accoutrements to a new gown. The house had been in an uproar for weeks preparing for Tabatha's debut. Such uproar that my arrival that day had been forgotten, hence the ill-fated taxi and my limited wardrobe. So I suppose I had a practical reason, in addition to all my philosophical reasons, for disliking the debutante season. But tonight, I just wanted to avoid being called into Tabatha's room to comment on her attire. Not only would I inevitably insult my sister and all the women present, but I would be made very late for this, uh, engagement. That is what it was, an engagement.

"I'll be late," I shouted a premature defense and descended the stairs in haste.

Voices called out to me, "Where are you going? With whom? Don't forget—," but the rest was drowned out by the scream of my sister, most likely caused by a misguided pin piercing her skin.

I opened the front door and stepped into the thick night air, wearing a gray suit and collage of green-and-yellow golfers.

2

J ANE WAS DRIVING THE SAME OLD Alfa Romeo she had driven forever. It had been her uncle's, until he remarried and gave it to Jane. Seemed his new wife didn't think that a married man should be driving an Italian sports car. Not, in my opinion, a great way to start a marriage. I opened the door and hopped in.

Jane looked great—just enough black dress to cover what I feared I might never see again. It made her look like part of the sporty leather seat. "Couldn't come to the door, eh?"

"In this neighborhood?" she quipped and looked about cautiously at the handsomely kept frame houses with neat subtropical gardens boasting banana trees, impatiens, and ivy, all shaded by old oaks weary from their heavy burden of Spanish moss.

"Look at all those security system signs," she laughed. "Anyway, I didn't want to turn the engine off. I still have to push start it."

She was talking a lot and fast. She was nervous, but I could not imagine why. I was hardly the type to make women quiver.

I tried to put her at ease. "You look great," I said, aiming for sincerity but missing the mark badly.

"Thanks. I love your tie."

"It was the only one I have," I said, thinking there must be three ties in the suitcase the taxi driver left at the airport. I could have borrowed one from my father, but as my mother bought all his ties too, the result was not likely to be different. "It was a gift."

"From Mom?" She turned and looked at me, a move that showed more cleavage than I recalled. "So why did you call me?"

Still busy with her breasts, the question caught me off guard. I could only manage a shrug.

Jane interpreted my silence as a sign of trepidation and thoughtfully changed the subject, which was the decent thing to do. "I haven't heard from you in years."

Having remained quiet as long as one reasonably can, I was now obliged to provide an answer. "I suppose I was busy." It wasn't a very good answer, but it was all I could find.

"Busy?" Jane revved the engine, presumably to prevent the Alfa from stalling.

"Busy being engaged."

"Yes, I am sorry things didn't work out for you. Still, it does seem an awfully long time to be engaged." She revved the engine again, dropped the clutch, and we drove away from the house like bank robbers.

"What do you mean?" I asked, watching uptown New Orleans pass at high speed.

"Well, something was bound to go amiss in two years of engagement. Hell, most marriages don't last that long. And there you go stringing some young girl along for two years."

"She was not a young girl. She was a partner in a law firm, and the two years were her idea."

"Why did she want to wait?"

"God only knows. She was the one set on marriage. I went along for the ride."

The light at St. Charles Avenue turned red. Jane stopped the Alfa abruptly and turned toward me again, looking rather disappointed.

"The ride?" Jane asked.

"I mean that she orchestrated the whole thing. She wanted the two-year engagement. She wanted the big wedding."

"And you, what did you want?"

"How should I know? I wanted things to go smoothly."

"Smoothly?" she asked incredulously.

The light turned green. The car stalled.

"Shit," she said, banging both hands on the steering wheel. "I thought you were supposed to be lucky."

"Nope. My luck ran out years ago."

She opened her door and stepped out onto the street—black dress, pumps, and the horns of the impatient behind us.

"You want to help?" she asked, looking back into the car at me. I got out, unbuttoned my coat, and joined her.

"Really, Tim, five years in Boston has not helped your capacity to capture the essence of experience in language, has it?" Jane asked, with one hand against the open door pushing, the other on the wheel steering. I mentioned that it hadn't been five years, but she didn't notice and kept to her theme.

"Smoothly? I can't imagine what you might mean by smoothly. No engagement goes smoothly."

We were running now, having crossed the westbound lanes into the neutral ground.

"Smoothly isn't what engagements are about. Perhaps it was this desire for 'a smooth ride' that she sensed. A smooth ride! It sounds like you were less committed to her than you were to the ride. You think that was going through her mind when she decided to terminate the engagement?"

"How am I to know what was going through her mind?" I said, gasping for air.

"Did you ask her?" Jane slid back inside in a single, fluid motion, popped the clutch, and after a jerky grind of transmission, the Alfa choked, belched, started, and off they both went. At this point, I was no longer pushing but, rather, running to keep up. I was still running when Jane hit the brakes so I could get in. I collided with the open door, jamming my fingers against the window, and hit my head on the rooftop as I stumbled into the seat.

"I didn't think," I paused, wheezing, "it was necessary."

"What do you mean?"

"Didn't you hear?" I asked, not sure what she knew about my engagement. "She met somebody else."

"Heavens, no, I hadn't heard. I am sorry, terribly sorry. How tragic," she said with great sincerity.

"It wasn't really tragic—comic, in a sort of twisted way, but not tragic," I said, still straining to catch my breath.

"Are you OK?" she asked as we zoomed away from the scene.

"Perfect," I said, trying to compose myself. "It has just been a while since I've had to push start a car."

"You did fine," she assured and turned to look at me. "Are you sure you're OK?"

I nodded to avoid further embarrassing myself.

"You used to be in better shape. What's the matter? Boston living's made you soft or something?"

"It wasn't the pushing, it was the stopping," I said, gathering myself. I looked over at her again. She really looked great. I guess push starting her Alfa every day kept her young. I decided to tell her so. "You really look great. When I called you, I was a little afraid that you might have, uh, changed."

"That's what doing nothing will do to you."

"What's that?" I asked.

"Nothing."

I caught myself playing with the golf tie and put my hand in my coat pocket to stop. "Well, I am just glad to see you didn't fill in, so to speak, while I was away."

"Fill in?"

"One wonders," I said defensively, trying to decipher what the hell I was talking about.

"You've been wondering if I had filled in?" the last two words were spoken with scorn.

"Certainly not," I lied, again unconvincingly. The conversation was getting away from me.

"Would that have mattered?"

I wasn't really sure what she meant at this point, but I knew she was upset. I didn't want to upset her. I tried to fix it.

"Ah . . . no, I don't guess so. But you know, it's just strange to see someone after you haven't seen them for a long time and find out they are fat or pregnant or married . . ." as if marriage was the same as being fat. I was saying more than I intended and was trying to think of a way to end the sentence before I made things any worse. "And you just wonder." I failed.

"So are you still working at the Fair Grounds?" I hoped to steer the conversation into safer territory.

"No, I was fired."

"Fired?" I was not doing well. Before I left, Jane had a great job working at the racetrack, and in New Orleans, where the unemployment rate hovered around fifteen percent in the best of times, finding a full-time job with benefits straight out of college was a real coup. She had been the assistant to the track manager, which meant that she was involved in virtually every aspect of the business of racing horses. Our families were well acquainted, but I had gotten to know Jane intimately through my regular visits to the Fair Grounds while I was a graduate student at Tulane. And though I was loath to admit it, she had been the key to my success at the track. "What happened?"

"My boss and I had a difference of opinion."

"What difference?"

"He thought my job included sleeping with him."

"And you didn't."

"It didn't pay that much."

"So what have you been doing since then?"

"Nothing. There are no jobs in this city."

"Is that why you are living at home?"

She shrugged. "It isn't so bad."

"You could have moved to another city. There are jobs in Boston. It's a great town." I hoped this didn't sound like a proposal.

Jane scoffed but said nothing, apparently focusing on driving, which could not have been easy. The windows were so dirty I couldn't see a thing, except the occasional red brake lights of the cars that seemed only an accident away. "How can you see out of these windows?"

"I can't."

That didn't make me feel any better. I rolled down my window. I couldn't see where we were going, but at least I could see what we were passing, the stone library and white frame houses that had been there forever. She was right, nothing here had changed. She slowed as we approached the light at Napoleon Avenue.

"Where are we going?" I asked.

"I thought you would want to go to The Columns first?"

"Of course, but isn't there someplace new we might try?"

"No." She stopped at the red light. I stared out the window, admiring the beautiful, old Presbyterian church off to the right, its white columns and neat, red brick contrasting sharply with the heaving sidewalks and potholed streets of uptown. "I thought you would like to visit The Mermaid later tonight."

"The Mermaid?"

"You remember it."

"Has it changed?"

"No."

"Then why go?"

"Oh, come on, it will be fun. That all-girl band is playing. I figured you would want to see that."

"Oh Christ. Are they still alive?"

"As bad as ever."

"Do they still do that chicken song?"

"Last I heard."

"Is there any way to avoid it?"

"No."

The light changed. The car stalled.

3

THE TOWERING COLUMNS that framed the expansive veranda overlooking St. Charles Avenue gave the hotel its name. I was glad to see that, like everything else, The Columns Hotel hadn't changed: a half-dozen round tables surrounded by wrought iron chairs, flags hanging from the balcony above, and a quaint little garden with fountains, benches, and a couple of tables off to the side. Jane parked the car around the corner. It was December, but it was still warm enough to sit outside. We took a table on the almost empty front porch overlooking the garden. Another couple, dressed as if on a date, sat together by the steps, sipping champagne cocktails from tall, thin glasses, and four men in shirts and ties occupied a table near the entrance to the hotel. I could hear Brazilian jazz coming from inside. The barmaid appeared almost immediately, as if she had been hovering just behind the door. I started with beer. Jane ordered a Sazerac with "just a dash of sugar."

The barmaid was clearly surprised by the request.

"Did you say 'Sazerac'?"

Jane nodded, and the barmaid disappeared, but not before giving me a strange look. It was a look of disapproval that asked, "Who orders like that?" Perhaps I was reading too much into it. I was never good at reading people. Jane was.

"It is not a complicated drink," she said to me after the barmaid was gone. "You would think I had asked for a gin fizz." She sighed dramatically. "There are so few places in the city that do anything more than pour beer or make well drinks. It's all bourbon and Coke, rum and Coke, Seven and Seven. I chose The Columns because you used to drink martinis. It is the only place uptown that makes a decent martini."

"I don't drink them much anymore."

"How did it happen?"

"It's too cold in Boston to drink martinis. Mostly folks there drink beer."

"No, I mean how did your fiancée meet someone else?"

"Oh, that. Margaret's a Catholic," I said.

"Because she is Catholic she met somebody else?"

"No, I mean she is a real Catholic, a Boston Catholic, a real believer, not the atheist sort of Catholic we were all raised to be."

"I didn't know there was a difference," Jane smiled.

"I didn't either."

"And all Boston Catholics are real believers?" she asked, lifting a skeptical eyebrow at me.

"I can't be sure. I make that judgment based on a small sample size."

"How small?"

"My fiancée."

"That's pretty small."

"How many Catholic girls from Boston must I propose to before I am afforded some prejudice on the matter?"

Jane shook her head at me knowingly. "I don't suppose you can be expected to deploy the scientific method."

"My prejudices are based on a case study."

"And how did this real Catholicism case manifest itself?"

"She went away on a weeklong retreat, a silent retreat, a 'spiritual renewal' she called it, something she had wanted to do for years. They have some name for it, but I can't recall what."

"So?"

"So she got renewed all right. Met some guy. They fell in love."

"Fell in love? At a silent retreat? How?"

"You got me. Five days in silence, nothing but prayer, meditation, and mass, and they were in love."

"Were they alone?"

"Nope, the place had some fifty other retreaters and was crawling with silent monks and quiet priests."

"Quiet priests?"

"Yeah, I guess they can only talk at mass."

"And that is the official name for these semi-silent priests?"

"Oh no, I just made the name up myself."

"Clever." The barmaid arrived with my beer and Jane's Sazerac. "So a week of silence and they were in love, eh?"

"How do you fall in love in five days?"

"Maybe when you don't talk so much, the relationship progresses faster," she said with another sly smile that was a cross between flirting and sarcasm. I couldn't read her.

"I don't know, but they got engaged."

"That must have hurt. No wonder you didn't tell anyone."

"Tell anyone what?"

"Margaret's breaking off the engagement for some other guy."

"Yeah, I guess so. I don't know. I didn't think that anyone would believe it. Fortunately, I hadn't told too many folks that I was engaged at all."

"Yes, I know. You never told me. Naturally, my mother eventually heard."

"I would have told you myself," I defended, "but what do you say? 'I am engaged to be married in a few years'? It sounds ridiculous."

"Have you dated anyone since then?"

"No," I said unconvincingly. It was true, and I sounded like I was lying.

"What? I figured with all that Southern charm, you'd have to chase them off up there." Jane broke her gaze and glanced downward at her Sazerac.

"I guess they prefer the silent type," I said, taking a healthy swallow of the watery beer.

"Then why didn't you ever call or write me? All I got was a lousy Christmas card after you disappeared, and it didn't arrive until the middle of January."

I couldn't believe that she remembered that stupid card—and that it was late.

"Your timing was beautiful. Just a day after my mother had cleared the mantle of all the Christmas cards, she finds yours in the mailbox." Jane raised her eyebrows accusingly. She had beautiful eyes. "Had I discovered it, I would have thrown it away immediately, but you know my mother. She has some odd affinity for mail. She has boxes of old letters in the attic."

"Don't you save letters?" I asked.

"For a few days, if I intend to read them again, but I rarely do read them again even when I intend to. I suppose the only reason I keep them is because my mother panics when she sees me read a letter and then throw it in the trash. She always asks if it was bad news, and I always tell her no, and then she doesn't believe me and later digs it out of the trash in search of some evidence of human suffering." She paused, raised her cocktail to her lips, reconsidered, and set it down. My mouth felt particularly dry, but my beer was finished. I resorted to staring into my mug.

"Anyway, she opens up your tacky reindeer card, because you didn't have the guts to address the envelope to me but instead to the whole damn family, even though it was a load of sappy crap about missing me. Imagine my shock when I found it on the mantle, a lonely Christmas card in the middle of January. I tried to throw it away twice but was informed that I had no right. The card created quite a scene. Everyone in the family had the pleasure of reading about how cold it was up there without me. My mother thought it was so charming that she left it there nearly a month. She always liked you, even though I explained that you had only written the damn thing out of guilt after having forgotten about me until you received my card. After that humiliation, I vowed never to write you again." She finally took a sip of her drink.

"I thought you were mad about Helen," I said in defense of my tardiness, but my timing was off again. Had I known how funny Jane would find this comment, I would have held it until she had swallowed. I had been in earnest, but she nearly drowned right there at the table in a spectacle that I feared would prompt someone to dial 911. But she was not to be deterred. In the midst of her coughing-choking-laughter, she regained her composure for an instant.

"You thought that I was mad about . . . Helen?" She had to whine to get the name Helen out before the laughter returned, along with the coughing.

"Yeah, well, maybe I hoped you were mad about her. I don't know. Anyway, that's why I didn't send you a card earlier." At this point, I was inventing history. It wasn't that I was lying. It was simply that I did not remember what I had thought about Jane at the time. This is not to say I hadn't thought Jane. I had, constantly. My sister Sarah called this trait "insensitivity." I preferred to think of it as a bad memory. It had been three years, well, two since the letter, but I didn't feel like I could tell Jane that I couldn't remember what I felt at the time. I tried it to myself: "Jane, I don't remember what I thought about you after I sent the letter." It sounded insensitive, arrogant, and obnoxious. But this story about Helen seemed plausible. It is what I should have thought. And it is what I was thinking now. So then, it was probably what I had thought. Right?

Jane was still laughing when the barmaid arrived with another beer. I went at it directly.

"What ever happened to her anyway?" Jane asked, regaining her composure.

"I don't know."

"Did she have the baby?"

"No."

"Did that bother you?"

"Not really. I mean, not that way."

"What way?" she pressed.

"Well, I never really felt that paternal instinct, you know? One minute I hear she's pregnant, the next she's not. Maybe if I had been pregnant it would have been different, but for me it was as if the whole thing had been nullified, as if the entire evening had been cleanly wiped from history. That's what seemed strange to me."

"I don't follow you." She did not look convinced.

"I mean that it was like nothing had ever happened. The waving of a medical glove was like the forgiveness of a priest. All my sins were absolved. The error of an evening removed from my permanent record. The mistake was fixed. Nothing had happened."

"What's wrong with that?"

"Nothing, I guess." I paused, drank, and looked across St. Charles Avenue for answers. "It made me feel impotent."

"Impotent?" she said with a Sazerac smile.

"Yeah, like nothing I do will ever be of any consequence, right or wrong. I mean, if I can do something as stupid as that and suffer no consequences from it, I might as well not be alive."

"Did you pick this up in Boston?"

"What?"

"Your new existentialism."

"I think it's the company."

"You sound like all those silly women at Bryn Mawr."

"Were they existentialists?"

"No, feminists," Jane added with a smile.

"And you aren't?" I asked. I had always loved her feisty, iconoclastic mode of feminism.

"Not in the Bryn Mawr mold, I am not. They made everything political. Even body hair was political. If you shaved your legs, you were oppressing women."

"Did you shave your legs?"

"Yes."

"And to think your mother was concerned you would be intimidated by all those intellectual girls."

"I never fit in. At Bryn Mawr, feminism was a tired, humorless personality the girls wore like a badge, a badge that screamed—"

"Would you like another, sir?" interrupted the barmaid, catching us both by surprise.

"Huh?"

"Would you like another?"

"Bourbon, please." I hadn't noticed any effects from the beer yet and was tired of not noticing what I was drinking. "A double, please."

"And you, ma'am?" she said, turning to Jane.

Jane nodded calmly. "But not so much sugar in this one, please," she said softly.

"What is the point of a Sazerac without the sugar?" I asked.

"Why, the absinthe, of course."

4

JANE SMILED AND TURNED toward the couple drinking champagne. "Don't they look content?" she asked without looking back at me.

"I think it's the champagne cocktails. They've had a steady stream of them since we arrived. But they will feel differently in the morning." I thought there was more truth in this than should be said in mixed company, so I tried to remedy it. "Champagne exacts a high price in the morning."

"You're as romantic as a toad," she said, turning to me. "A stupid toad. They look perfectly delightful."

The barmaid arrived with our drinks as well as fresh ones for the delightful couple, who hadn't yet reached the regretful stage. Jane tasted her Sazerac and smiled at the barmaid. "Thank you," she said and then, turning to me, asked, "Who have you seen since you've been back?"

"My family."

"How is everyone?"

"Standard state of chaos, I am happy to report."

"Nothing exotic?"

"Nothing beyond the norm. Of course, the whole house has been turned upside down with my sister's debut, and with her first ball tomorrow night, even the relatives are being sucked into the debutante season vortex," I said and sampled my bourbon.

"Who is there?"

"Well, my Aunt Page has been staying with us to take care of my mother."

"Your mother?"

"Yes, it is all quite brilliant—the thinking really exceeds the imagination. It goes something like this: My mother and sister Sarah are busy getting Tabatha ready for her debut. But they are so busy with Tabatha that they need caring for themselves, and so enter the aunts. Page has been there some time now, and my Aunt Dee will be arriving from Baton Rouge tomorrow. Of course, the arrival of all these aunts creates an intense amount of work for my mother, getting the house ready, so she has asked me to come supervise the household during the debutante season."

"And this explains your visit?"

"Not at all. I had every intention of visiting this Christmas. I haven't been back here in quite some time. No, it only explains my mother paying for the airline ticket."

"And what about your father?"

"He goes into hiding during these events. It seems that he is constantly saying the wrong thing at the wrong time and sending all the women into tears, and so he disappears. I haven't seen him yet myself."

"Incredible. But he will be at the ball tomorrow?"

"Naturally. My mother makes him study all the times and dates of the various engagements that he must attend and then still requires that he keep a schedule in his pocket and his tuxedo in the trunk of his car throughout the season."

"What a sophisticated woman she is. Does it work?"

I shrugged and finished my bourbon. Jane was still nursing her second Sazerac. I looked around for the barmaid, but she was at the men's table next to the entrance. They looked like they were having trouble explaining what they wanted. I suspected they were feigning confusion to flirt with her. She was lovely.

Jane interrupted my observation. "So in the house right now, there is Tabatha, Sarah, your mom, your dad—presumably hiding somewhere out of sight—you, an aunt, and another aunt arriving tomorrow?"

"Yes, I believe that's it. But they will all be gone in a few weeks—all but Sarah."

"Yeah, I heard she had moved back home."

"Looks like she is home for good."

"What about Patrick? Aren't they still married?"

"I suppose. I can't really say. You know Sarah. You'll have to ask her."

"Didn't you ask her?"

"Yeah, but I couldn't understand what she was saying. Something about agoraphobia, I don't know."

"Fear of open spaces?"

"Fear of reality is more accurate. Sarah has always been controlled by her fears, and those fears have always been numerous. You know, she checked herself into a mental hospital when she was seventeen."

"I didn't know."

"An ugly little family secret. My mother was beside herself, though I am not sure if it was from concern for Sarah or from embarrassment."

"What was wrong with her?"

"Nothing, or at least nothing the doctors could find. They said she had done it to get attention. My mother was mortified. My brother called her 'psycho-Sarah' for years afterward, which probably didn't help her feeble grip on reality."

"I have heard him call her that. I thought it was because she sounds like Norman Bates."

"She does sound like Norman Bates."

"How is your brother? Have you seen him?" she asked and signaled the barmaid to bring me another drink. The barmaid nodded her understanding as she delivered martinis to the men's table.

"He's getting married." There was a moment of silence. She just sat there and stared at me, as if I was supposed to say something more. But I had just said that the bastard was getting married. What the hell more could there be? "He called me last night and insisted I go downtown to see him as soon as I arrived. He had news he couldn't tell me over the phone. So I had the cab from the airport drop me off at his favorite coffee shop."

"Starbucks?"

"The Walmart of coffee shops."

"It's very Seattle," Jane laughed.

"It's very stupid. I had to wait in line for thirty minutes to buy a cup of coffee that cost three dollars. I could go to a restaurant, sit down, and be served a better cup of coffee for half the price in a tenth the time." Jane was drinking more steadily now. I presumed she was bored with my diatribe on Starbucks or she was making room for the coming drinks. I returned to my story. "So I wait thirty minutes for a cup of bad coffee and another thirty minutes at a table for my lousy brother, and the bastard never shows up. So there I am, in the coffee shop, with my luggage and a bad cup of three-dollar coffee. I called him at his office, and he said he'd gotten stuck in an important meeting. Then he tells me over the phone he is getting married." I paused for a taste of bourbon, but there was only ice left in the glass, so I chewed on that instead. With the ice in my mouth, I said, "He could have told me over the phone and saved me the cab fare downtown from the airport. But I did enjoy the streetcar ride home. The city is pretty this time of year."

"Wasn't somebody going to pick you up at the airport?"

"No, they are all too busy with Tabatha's debut. And William, he sure isn't going to take time off of work to come pick me up but expects me to go downtown to see him. He gives me all this 'Brothers have to talk brother to brother' and 'We're Schmidts . . . Schmidts are good people, it's what good people do' shit."

"And why didn't you just tell him no?"

"Have you ever tried to tell my brother no?"

"Yes."

"Did it work?"

"No," she whispered.

"Exactly. And he has become so very proper now. He used to be a shiftless good-for-nothing. Then he sneaks through law school at Loyola. Either their standards have dropped or he cheated his way through. Then my dad helps land him this cushy DA job downtown, and all of a sudden he thinks he's the Prince of Wales."

The barmaid returned with my drink. Her age was startling, but only to me. She was quite young—something I never saw in Boston. The impact of Louisiana's subtle resistance to the twenty-one-year-old drinking age was only now starting to impress me. By strictly enforcing an older drinking age, the other forty-nine states had only increased the value of a fake ID and eliminated the beautiful, young barmaid as a cultural phenomenon. That's what I hated about drinking in Boston. The waitresses were old and jaded—hell, they had to be after interrogating every patron for certificates of authenticity. It was amazing how such a little change in the law could bring about such a massive transformation in the aesthetic of something so simple as drinking bourbon.

"Bourbon," she said, placing the glass in front of me and then lighting the small candle in the middle of the table. She walked thoughtfully to the next table and leaned over the chairs to light the candles there. This action drew her skirt tightly around her waist and revealed the slender youth of her body. I suppose I was staring.

"Pretty, huh?"

"What?" I said, turning away from my sin. "Yeah, well, I don't know. It's just that in Boston—"

"You don't have pretty girls?"

"Not like that," which was not at all what I meant, but it was all the bourbon would let out. I considered trying to explain myself, explain Boston, explain the social horrors of drinking laws, and explain the beauty of the nubile barmaid, but it was done. The words wouldn't come. The ideas were fading too. It was an alcoholic epiphany, and like a dream, you could never fully recreate its genius.

Inside The Columns, the band struck up "Corcovado," and thinking that a brief change of scene might improve my conversational skills, or at least conceal them, I asked her to dance. Jane was willing enough, though she did not seem eager to leave her drink. She hesitated, trying to decide whether to finish it or bring it along. She brought it with her, gripping it firmly in one hand, while holding the other out so that I might lead her to the ballroom. I abandoned my bourbon and took her hand.

5

WE WALKED THROUGH THE CORRIDOR on the first floor of The Columns Hotel, which was surrounded by a cluster of three rooms and eventually led to a registration desk and a winding stairwell. The largest of these rooms sported a splendid wooden floor and served as a ballroom whenever there was a band. Across from it, the two smaller rooms functioned as lounges. The first, boasting heavy, red upholstered chairs, was rarely ever used. The second was far more rustic and popular, with booths, couches, coffee tables, and a long bar at the rear. On this night, all three rooms were uncharacteristically crowded, probably because the band was unusually good.

There was a long, dark elderly woman in a black dress playing piano and singing; a fat, pale man playing guitar, sitting on what must have been for him, a very uncomfortable stool; and an inconspicuous little man in the back who appeared to be nodding off but would occasionally stir to play a few notes on his saxophone. A curious combination that worked splendidly. Everyone in the ballroom was either listening or dancing.

Jane took the lead and, with drink in hand, maneuvered us quickly into the crowd of bodies moving slowly and not very rhythmically across the floor. Without saying a word, she turned and buried herself into me. It was an awkward dancing position: her arms wrapped tightly around my neck, her nose tucked gently under my chin, and the rest of her body pressed firmly against mine as if she were trying to cover me or cover herself with me. I could not have been happier. We moved very slowly, listening to the music more than dancing to it. She whispered something. I couldn't make it out. I didn't care. I didn't want to talk. I just wanted to dance, if you could call it dancing. I didn't care what it was called. It was the best thing that had happened to me in ages, and I didn't want it to end.

The band moved on to another Brazilian favorite, "Desafinado." Some of the dancers retreated to the barroom for refills. I stayed close to Jane. I felt her lips move against my neck. Was she kissing me? It was intoxicating. I wanted to see her face, so that I could kiss her. But to pull away would be to disengage her lips from my neck, which I was not eager to do. I tried to do it gently, to sustain the embrace, to move her lips upward along my neck, to my chin, and finally to my mouth. But her head was locked under my chin. I would have to make a more aggressive move. I drew back slightly, just enough so that I could see her face. I just wanted to kiss her, there, in The Columns Hotel, in the rarely used ballroom, listening to an unlikely Brazilian jazz band. I wanted to kiss her, and at the risk of sounding like a romantic, I wanted that kiss to last forever.

I completed the disentanglement, leaving her arms around my neck and her lips vulnerable to mine, but Jane suddenly wanted to talk.

"So what about your brother?" Jane asked.

"My brother?" I was stunned. She went from kissing me on the neck to asking about my brother? Or, perhaps, she had never been kissing me at all. Perhaps all that kissing had merely been a one-sided conversation, made so by the Brazilian jazz and my imagination.

"Yeah."

I wanted to be furious, but most of her body was still pressed tightly against mine, and this contact acted like a powerful sedative for my meaner emotions. Still, I was not pleased with the subject matter.

"What about him?" I asked in a whiny tone that was unclear whether it was feeling sorry for itself or expressing anger. I focused on the angry part and continued. "The miserable bastard's getting married in a month. Can you believe it? A month. Who gets married in a month?"

Jane freed her Sazerac hand from our embrace, lifted the glass to her lips, but didn't drink, as if waiting for me to say something more, to finish my thought.

"OK, maybe two years is too long, but one month? Why wait at all if you are only going to wait a month? I mean, I don't give a shit how anybody gets married, but this is my brother we're talking about, Mr. William Martin Schmidt, Mr. Tradition, Mr. I'm-Gonna-Be-a-Pillar-in-the-Community. My mother will die. She will simply die. I can hear her already. 'Who ever heard of being engaged for just a month? It isn't done. People will think that the bride is pregnant, or worse.'"

"Or worse?" Jane asked and finished her drink. We weren't dancing anymore. We weren't even pressed together. I was trying to maintain my end of the conversation, but all I could think about was what a mistake it had been to try and kiss her. I should have simply enjoyed the moment. Idiot.

"I threw that in for flair," I said. "You know how my mother is. Anyway, she probably will try and stop the wedding. I can't image her allowing it."

"Why not?"

"I don't know, but for Christ's sake, he hasn't even told her yet. I told him it would be better to just elope, but he would have none of it. He insists that he and his girl have been planning it for quite a while now but simply haven't gotten around to telling anyone. Technically, he says he has been engaged for months."

"Would that make it OK?"

"Hell if I know what goes for OK around here any-more. I come home to find my sister Sarah living at home and my brother preparing to announce a one-month engagement. My sisters have always been odd, and my mother probably expected something like this from Sarah, but you have got to understand that William is in an entirely different league as far as my parents are concerned. Since he graduated from law school, he has become even more the stalwart of decency who has always enabled my parents to endure the disappointments Sarah and I have brought them. He was the first, the best looking, the best athlete, and after

law school, the most successful." I paused, desperately
wanting another drink. "I don't see my mother going
for the whole thing. She's going to think he knocked
her up."

"Her?"

"His fiancée."

"He didn't say who she is?"

"No."

"And you didn't ask?"

"No."

"Why not?"

"I figured I don't know her anyway, so why should
I care?"

"But what if you do know her?"

"Who do I know who would willingly marry my
brother? I can only imagine it must be someone he
met at one of these debutante parties. He goes to them
religiously. He is always invited."

"I once heard your mother call him 'uptown's most
eligible bachelor.'"

"Yes, well, I think he gave himself the title. Anyway,
he is always boasting about how all the young girls hang
on him."

"So you think his fiancée is younger than he is?"

"I don't know. I don't even know how old my brother
is anymore."

"He's three years older than you."

"You mean he's thirty-three?"

Jane nodded while raising her eyebrows at my ignorance.

"Is that all? I thought he was forty at least. No, no
eighteen-year-old debutante would marry him. She

might sleep with him—imagine that—but not marry him. No, at eighteen a girl still has dreams, and there is something about William that would stifle any dream anyone might have. Frankly, Jane, I don't care who he marries, or if she is pregnant as hell, or worse, as long as I don't have to take part."

"Take part?"

"He asked me to be his best man."

Jane stared at her glass but found it empty again. "I don't see your girlfriend," she said, looking around the room. The band had stopped; perhaps they were taking a break. "I need another drink."

"Girlfriend?"

"Yeah, the cute one bringing us drinks."

I frowned.

"Let's go back to our table. Perhaps I can get one there."

The barmaid arrived just as we did and took our request for another round.

"There was a bourbon on the table when we left," I said to the barmaid.

"The busboy probably drank it," she said as she retreated. I hadn't seen a busboy, but I didn't doubt her story. I had learned to drink while working as a busboy and was confident I had not started the tradition.

Jane opened her purse and started hunting for something. Eventually she produced a crumpled pack of cigarettes, extracted two of them, and lit them both with the candle on the table. She handed me one, took a deep breath of the other, and asked in a cloud of smoke, "So, what's so bad about being his best man?"

"Oh please," I said, fanning the smoke from my face, "I don't even like the bastard, never have. We never got along as kids and less so over the last ten years. We have played at being brothers our whole lives. He never even asked about Boston. He has never called or written. Probably doesn't even know what city I live in. And now all of a sudden he wants me to be his best man?"

"What did you say?" she asked, holding her cigarette away from the table.

"I didn't know what to say. I wanted to say that I felt sorry for any girl who got stuck with a guy who acted like he was forty when he was twelve. It's like he ages in dog years or something. He's thirty-three now, that's two hundred and thirty-one to you and me."

"So, what will you do?"

I shrugged my shoulders. "I certainly don't want to get involved in this big, uptown wedding he has planned, especially if his bride is showing. I just couldn't witness the song and dance of respectability that my family would feel obligated to perform. Everyone will know the truth, and everyone will pretend like nobody else knows, and everyone will speculate endlessly about the way such things ought to be handled." I slowed down and caught my breath. "That's why I left this place and went to work for my uncle in Boston."

"You left because you got Helen pregnant." By the tone of her voice, I expected her sentence to end with "you son of a bitch."

"Maybe so," I said, after a brief look for our barmaid and our drinks, "but you can see how the two are the same. My mother would have gone through the ceiling and then tried to fix everything."

"Fix Helen's pregnancy?"

"The whole thing. That's her style. Nothing goes wrong in my family. She always has a graceful and decent solution."

"What about the abortion?"

"That's not exactly a decent solution to my mother."

"Lots of uptown girls have abortions. Helen wasn't the first."

"Sure they do. Or they disappear for six months, 'visiting a relative,' my aunt used to say, or some such tale of adventure. One girl dropped out her senior year at Holy Name to go on a four-month rafting trip in southern France. Then these girls make a surprise return for the debutante season. Next thing you hear is that they are marrying some old high school sweetheart. Usually some pimply faced fellow whose parents are glad to see he will be settling down with a respectable girl." The barmaid arrived, which was a great relief to me. All this truth-telling had me parched. I set to the bourbon immediately. "I guess I didn't want my family involved. They want everything to be done right, to be done honorably. Some things aren't honorable, no matter how you disguise it."

"So you left."

"Seemed like the thing to do at the time."

"How cavalier. I guess you avoided honor that way."

"I never claimed to be honorable. But at least it wasn't a farce."

"What about Helen?"

I sighed and stared into space the way I always did when answering that question. I had given the answer to myself a thousand times late at night, or while riding the train to work, or at work when things were just droning on, and it was always the same. The problem was that I had never actually given it to a person. Jane sat silently waiting. I waited. Nothing happened. I drank more bourbon. Still, nothing happened. I decided to try something new.

"What difference does it make now?" I didn't know where I was going with this, but I was tired of the old answer I had been telling myself for years.

"None, I guess."

"I had no reason to stay here." Again, I was describing feelings about which I had no recollection. Somehow, I had just left. Why I left, or what I was feeling when I left, was a mystery to me now. I could probably give reasons about my decision, but I suspect the reasons I would give now would not be identical to the reasons I had three years ago. I tried not to think about it. I put out the cigarette that I had never touched and drank the remainder of the bourbon. I never cared for cigarettes, but the bourbon was finally serving its purpose, blurring the sharp edges from the world.

"What about me?" she asked and looked away. She was trying something even newer, something I was wholly unprepared for.

"You?" I choked out.

"Yeah, me, idiot," she said, looking back at me. "You never even told me that you were leaving. It was so embarrassing. I called your house and asked to speak with you, only to have your mother tell me you were in Boston. She gave me your address and phone number, but I wasn't about to call you."

My hands began to shake, and I wasn't sure why. "Didn't you know about Helen and me?"

"That y'all were sleeping together?" she said with a trace of sarcasm. "I think even my grandmother knew." She was maintaining her cool far better than I.

"It was only once," I corrected.

"Well, that's the only part that is news to me."

"Then I was right."

"Right about what?"

"That you knew about Helen and me."

"So?"

"So," I tried to rein in my emotions by taking a slow sip of bourbon, but, again, I found it empty. The familiar motion helped a little anyway. I looked away and saw the barmaid delivering more champagne cocktails. Our friends would be in rough shape tomorrow. I signaled for more bourbon. "I know you and I were really just friends and all, but we had, uh," I faltered and couldn't go on. I took a long sip of ice and looked her in the eyes.

"Sex?" she finished for me and stared, challenging me to say something intelligent.

I tried. "So I just figured that you would be pissed about Helen." I failed.

"You keep saying that. You sound like a broken record. A bad broken record. A bad, whiny broken record, *The Best of The Smiths*, or something."

"OK, I get it," I said. My voice was beginning to squeak a bit from the bourbon. But I really didn't get it. I understood the record motif but not the part about Helen. Jane tried to speak but stopped herself. Was she going to tell me that she loved me? I was scared to death, because if she did, I would end up regretting the last three years of my life, regretting leaving New Orleans, regretting leaving the one girl I really loved, regretting everything. I loved her now more than ever, but to proclaim it seemed absurd, especially after that awkward effort at a kiss. These thoughts were made harder by the haze of brown liquor and my general distrust of my own emotional intelligence. I tried to concentrate. I would tell her. I would tell her now, but I needed a drink to steel myself to it. Where was that eighteen-year-old barmaid?

"Tim, Jane, what are you doing here?" I turned around to see a bourbon-blurred figure whose voice was so obviously my brother's. He was accompanied by another fellow who seemed to linger in the background. William introduced us, but the name didn't stick. Then he turned to Jane and said, "And this is the lovely lady I have been going on about all night."

The background fellow said something. I didn't catch it.

My brother said something.

Jane said something.

I heard my brother's voice again.

"What?" I asked, twisting my head around trying to clear the effects of my growing inebriation, even if just for a moment. I needed a second to think. "Wait!"

"Wait?" he asked, laughing. "What, all those years in, uh, the North, and you can't handle your liquor anymore?" I knew he didn't know where I lived. I wanted to throw up. I wanted to stand up and punch him right in the nose, but I wanted to throw up more. I looked at Jane. She looked trapped, helpless, like a dog on the neutral ground in heavy traffic. And I was trapped too. William kept talking, like he always did. I couldn't understand him, but his voice kept coming and that voice made it impossible to think. I wanted to tell him to shut up.

"What are you doing here?" I asked him. It just came out. I didn't care what he was doing there. It just came out.

"We've been inside all evening. One of the partners had a little birthday party tonight and . . ." He could have talked all night. Perhaps he did. Another bourbon magically appeared. I drank it. William continued to speak. Goddamn, he could talk. "I hope you're looking after her for me tonight."

I turned to Jane. She turned away and stared off toward St. Charles Avenue.

"Anyway, I wish we could join you, but . . ." I guess he said something about the other fellow having to be home or something. Anyway, he went on in endless detail apologizing and explaining why he couldn't stay. I was thankful when he shook my hand to leave.

William kissed Jane good-bye. She seemed ambivalent, but maybe it was the bourbon that made me think so. I could feel the blood rush to my face, not sure if it was caused by my overindulgence or the kiss I had just witnessed. Then he was gone.

There was silence.

The silence was painful. It was the kind of pain that comes only from the unhappy combination of alcohol and tragedy, the kind that answers only to more alcohol. I cast about haphazardly for the barmaid and accidentally met Jane's eyes.

Then clarity, the haze was gone.

6

TWO MORE DRINKS CAME. I suppose someone had ordered them. I lifted my glass. Jane lifted hers as well and finally looked at me. I drank. She set hers back on the table, untouched.

"You're pregnant."

"Yes," she said, but didn't turn away this time. She was looking at me as if I were naked, as if I should be embarrassed. I felt embarrassed. I didn't know why I felt embarrassed. Because I had tried to kiss my brother's pregnant fiancée? No, that wasn't it. The bourbon wouldn't allow me full access to my own feelings. I still had the feelings, I just couldn't understand them. I was mad that she was pregnant, but who was I to be angry about her being pregnant? She wasn't my fiancée, girlfriend, lover. She was just a friend. I suppose I was embarrassed by my anger. I had no right to be angry, but I was.

"You shouldn't be drinking," I said, in a weak effort to express these new feelings.

"Shut up!" she yelled, probably attracting more than a few stares, though I didn't look around to check as I might normally have done.

"You can't marry him." I was angry.

"Why not?" she responded like a pit viper.

"You don't love him."

"Perhaps. Perhaps he doesn't love me. I don't know. How can we ever know?" She seemed to perk up a bit and suddenly was cheerful, as if the symmetry of it made it pleasant. "But he's got such a sense of, oh, what is it?"

"Crap."

"Honor, I suppose he would say."

"Honor? You call that honor?"

"You're just jealous."

"Perhaps. But not of him."

"Have you ever considered the possibility that the antagonism between you two is your fault?"

"Yes, I have."

"And?"

"And I concluded that it was his fault." I drank and went on the offensive. "You could just get an abortion."

"Abortion? Do people in Boston talk like that? I am pregnant, for Christ's sake. You don't just tell a pregnant woman to have an abortion."

"Oh, come now. You may be silly enough to marry my brother, but you can't have bought that pro-life line already. Any moral code that forces a person to marry my brother can't be called pro-life." I paused. "You would have to call it pro-death." The phrase seemed quite clever when it came to me in mid-sentence, but it didn't sound as clever when I said it. The bourbon was taking its toll on my wit. Don't try to be witty, I told myself.

"No, Tim, I won't have an abortion. It might have been easy enough two months ago. Hell, had I been smart about it, nobody would have known. Maybe even William wouldn't have known. But I couldn't pretend that nothing happened. I couldn't pretend I was still the perfect, uptown girl, pure as, as," she was struggling now too, "as whatever the hell is still pure in this world. I just can't think of anything."

She paused, bit her lip, and tried to recover her senses. "I've never been good at pretending. I saw what it did to you. I saw what it did to Helen."

"You've seen Helen?" I asked, now realizing that she had orchestrated much of this conversation.

"Only once. She married."

I finished my bourbon. "Who?"

"Do you care?"

"No." I lifted the glass of ice to my lips and drank air.

"She didn't seem to either. Married a lawyer. Guy named Thompson."

"Is she happy?"

She shrugged. "What do you think?"

"So why marry my brother, for Christ's sake? How can you pretend to be happy with that?"

"Whom would you have me marry?" she asked, mindlessly stabbing the burned-out cigarette that had been sitting harmlessly in the ashtray. She had only tasted it once, but she put it out with a vengeance.

Drunk as I was, I knew better than to answer that. I just looked away and shrugged my shoulders.

She exhaled deeply and hung her head a bit in an uncharacteristic sign of weakness. "I don't know what to do."

She toyed with her drink some more, tilting it to and fro, but never actually lifting it from the table.

"It was easy for you, Tim. You just ran away." She was getting worked up again. "You saved yourself, and you saved everybody else. You played the role of the perfect, Southern gentlemen, running off to the North to seek his fortune." She seemed angry. "You even played the role in Boston, didn't you?"

She didn't wait for me to answer.

"I know you did. Your mother told me you subscribed to *The Times-Picayune*," she was rambling. "It's just so cliché."

The Sazeracs had gotten to her, or perhaps she was just plain mad, mad at me. But why? What had I done? I hadn't gotten her pregnant. I hadn't even kissed her. I tried to defend myself.

"I just wanted to keep up with the Saints." What was I saying? Was I even in this conversation? I had never been very good with emotion, especially other people's emotions. This was definitely more emotion than I was prepared to deal with. I told myself to shut up again.

"You just wanted to maintain the façade. You say that you hate all this New Orleans shit, but you still live it. You proved that when you ran away. You could have dealt with Helen and just told your family to go to hell, but you ran away. Well, I can't do that. I haven't got an uncle in Boston or anywhere else. I can't be the perfect daughter anymore. But I can be a good mother."

"You don't have to marry William to be a mother."

"No, I don't. But he will be a good father. He has a job, a real job." This comment seemed aimed at me. "He'll make a good dad. That counts for something. It's real."

"So you're just going to marry him?"

"Yes."

"That's ridiculous. You're going to ruin your whole life, for one night." But I wasn't mad anymore. She was mad. I was now just a casual observer making unsolicited commentary.

"It wasn't just one night." She gave the barmaid a wave, pointing to my empty glass.

"You slept with him more than once?" I had assumed the first time had been alcohol induced, but to do it twice indicated a certain interest. It was one thing to like the idiot from afar. I could even understand a little physical desire. He is a handsome fellow. But to sleep with him once and then want to do it again? It didn't seem right. I tried for a moment to imagine Jane and William together. The image slowly took shape through the bourbon, and there it was. Surprisingly, I was not appalled by it. They were both attractive. Perhaps they were right for each other. But could she really love him? I guess it was possible. Terribly unlikely, but possible. I tried to erase the image, but it resisted. So there I sat, staring at Jane, imagining her in bed with my brother. It was annoying, like everything about my brother. It just annoyed me and wouldn't go away.

"I don't care," I said, not sure what I meant. I tried to clarify. "It's still stupid."

Another bourbon arrived. I was not sure I could keep at this pace and continue the conversation, but the arrival of the barmaid seemed to distract Jane. She sipped her Sazerac and made a face.

"Too sweet."

"A Sazerac is supposed to be sweet," I reminded her in a rather perfunctory way. I could still see her in bed with my brother. He was quite clumsy. I hoped I wasn't projecting.

"It's the absinthe, not the sugar, that makes the drink."

"So you said."

"The rye is already sweet enough. Adding all that sugar, it's disgusting."

"Like you and my brother getting married." The image was still there, and now, like a muse, it was inspiring me.

"And you're going to be standing there watching. Serves you right." Her anger was gone. Her sarcasm had returned. She had always enjoyed other people's misery over her own pleasure.

I just growled.

"You brother's best man," she sneered.

"I would rather die."

"Why? What difference does it make to you?"

"Oh please, you know how I feel."

I was disgusted, drunk, tired of seeing William and Jane in bed together, and ready to go home. The night had turned out to be a total failure. I thought about the upcoming debutante dance. I thought about returning to the comfort of Boston, to my little apartment in Somerville, to my tedious, little job at Marketing Records Management Services. My mind ran, ran from New Orleans.

"I don't know a thing about how you feel, Tim. I never have. You have never done anything to show me, ever."

"I made love to you, remember?" I looked for our barmaid. I wanted to flag her down, get the check, leave. This conversation was over.

"You also made love to Helen, remember?"

"That was different."

"How?"

"It was, and you know it."

"It wasn't. You only think it was because you never had to prove it wasn't. You had the chance to do something then, and you ran away. Now, you'll run away again. You'll leave again. I wonder if you will call in another five years."

"What am I supposed to do, ask you to run away with me in the night? Drag you to Boston with me, to be my lover, and raise my brother's child?" I was embarrassed to suggest it, and I was hoping the barmaid would arrive to rescue me from what had become an impossible discussion.

"You've done worse," she said.

I stopped searching for the barmaid and looked Jane directly in the eye. Was she serious or was she just being her old cynical self? What was she suggesting? The conversation was still impossible, but it had become interesting again.

"I'd better go. I've had too much to drink. I'm liable to say something I shouldn't."

"Now?" I was crushed.

"Yes."

I was crushed and confused.

"Your brother doesn't like me to drink too much—you know, the baby."

"You don't think this is too much?" I said, eyeing her still flat stomach.

"Considering the circumstances, no."

The barmaid arrived. Jane asked for the check. I fumbled for my wallet, while Jane got up and left without a word.

I looked up to watch her go, black dress, black shoes, black hair.

ANOTHER DATE

Our brighter young people are saturating
themselves today with a mass of knowledge that
can have little application for the lives which most
of them must inevitably lead. Disappointment and
discontent are almost sure to be the result.

Ellwood Cubberley

Scotch

4 OZ SCOTCH
1 TBSP WATER

Serve in a rocks glass over ice
or straight up.

7

I OPENED MY WALLET in search of large bills and a voice inside of me said, "You shouldn't have called her." I knew I would regret it. It would be dishonest to suggest that I had anticipated the cause or the profundity of my regret. I regretted everything: the date, my choice of attire, my return to New Orleans, and the monstrous hangover that would be my reward. I had long clung to the belief that a vigorous headache from a night of overconsumption demonstrates a healthy appetite for life, and it was a price I was generally willing to pay. But the cocktail cemetery on the table promised a desperate tomorrow. Though it is always perilous to contemplate the future while drunk, I began doing just that, perhaps in an effort to drive the image of Jane and my brother from my mind. The next twenty-four hours would bring breakfast with the family, a day of meeting and greeting distant relatives and family friends, some sort of dreadful luncheon, and finally the debutante ball. None of it sounded appealing, and I grimaced at the thought of squaring off against so many aunts and uncles, cousins, nephews, nieces, dressed and coiffed to a proper boil. People unaccustomed to the ritual of the debutante ball at least know the horrors of a wedding. The only real difference is that the debutante affair seems to have no particular purpose and seemingly no end, and this generally degrades the quality of the conversation, given that none of the participants knows exactly what's happening or even what is supposed to happen. It was hard enough to endure this image in my drunken state, but I was forced to imagine navigating the debutante events under the duress of an acute hangover. Mercifully, my reflections were interrupted by a great disturbance from inside the hotel.

"What do you mean my credit's no good here?" a disembodied voice shouted. "That's all I've got is credit. That's all anybody has is credit."

Silence. And then more shouting.

"You don't think those green slips of paper are worth anything, do you? It's credit. Just try eating one."

There was a crash and what sounded like pushing or perhaps falling.

"Credit? How can you question my credit when you serve swill like this? You call this Scotch? It is a credit to the constitution of your patrons that they can swallow the stuff, and it is a credit to some sniffly nosed marketing executive in New York City that he can convince you to sell the stuff, but it is no credit to this hotel."

This was followed by more sounds of pushing, and then the double doors to The Columns burst open as two massive, tuxedoed waiters shoved an even larger man in a houndstooth suit out onto the porch. It was an old houndstooth suit.

The waiters stopped and glared at the man. They were bent and breathing heavily.

"Leave now," the larger of the two waiters wheezed.

The suited man appeared undaunted. He was quite substantial, well over six feet tall and closer to three hundred pounds than two hundred. He took in a gulp of air as if to continue pontificating and then turned suddenly and stared at me.

"Tim?"

"No, I'm not paying for your Scotch," I said, placing a stack of twenty-dollar bills on the check and drinking what was left of my bourbon.

"Cash? Wow, you must be doing well up there in Boston."

The big fellow in the old suit walked over to me and plopped down in what had been Jane's seat. The two waiters were still staring at him.

"Put my drinks on his tab," he shouted and then reached into his pocket and drew out a long cigar. "Nice tie," he said, holding the cigar in a Churchillian fashion. "Do you have a light?"

I hesitated, but faced with the tuxedoed waiters, the bourbon burning in the back of my throat, the golfers tight around my neck, and the big man's cigar pointed at me, I succumbed, tossed two more twenties on the table, and passed him the candle centerpiece. "Nice to see you too, Milton."

"What the 'ell are you doing here? Never mind. I am really quite glad to see you."

He looked over his shoulder at the glaring waiters and decided to put the cigar back in his jacket.

"Do you mind a change of venue?" he asked in his odd, cockney accent. It was odd because he was originally from San Francisco. Doubtless it was affected, but he'd managed it as long as I had known him. With the threat of physical expulsion behind him, his accent returned to its full vigor.

"Now that you have gotten us excused from the only decent place in the city," I stood up and buttoned my coat, "where to?"

"Why, The Mermaid, of course," he said, spinning his great girth like a dancing hippo and walking dramatically toward the wide marble steps leading to the street.

Milton's splashy exit hadn't erased the memory of my date with Jane, but it did cast that failure in a new light. At least I hadn't been thrown out of the bar like Milton.

"Are you here alone?" I asked, noticing that my speech was improving. Standing up seemed to clear my head.

"Not anymore," he responded and chuckled to himself. "I am neither alone, nor am I 'here.'"

He stopped at the street and carefully looked both ways. He seemed to be searching for something.

"But if you are wondering, I do have an engagement this evening." He turned and stared at me. "A rather difficult engagement, or engagements, in fact, and it is for the sake of this, these engagements that I am glad to see you."

I looked away, perhaps betraying some mild disappointment. Milton had been my roommate and best friend in graduate school. I felt miserable and pathetic when Jane left me at The Columns. Milton's appearance was a splendid restorative.

"You don't need to break your engagements on my account. I'll be in town an entire month. We can catch up another time."

"Break them? Oh no. I don't intend to break them. On the contrary, I couldn't pull them off without some help. In fact, I was only here at The Columns hoping to gain some inspiration or perhaps run into someone like you."

He pointed to his left and started walking. "Come on."

I followed. "Are you planning to rob a bank?"

He looked at me callously and then smiled. "No. I have a date."

"Then I don't see why you need me."

"Well, not really a date, more like two dates."

I began to get nervous and was thinking of returning to The Columns and another glass of bourbon. "I don't follow you."

"Oh, it is quite easy really." He waved his hand in a flourish toward a yellowish car parked on the street. "Here it is."

"It" was a 1980s four-door K-car. An unhappy creature that was so terribly unfashionable, even in its prime. This particular specimen also looked to have been in at least one serious accident from which it had never recovered.

"Where did you find this?" I asked.

"What?"

I pointed at the car.

"Oh. I won it in a bet." He flashed me a generous smile that revealed his big teeth and rubbery lips.

"Are you sure you won?"

"Isn't she brilliant?" Milton opened the driver's side door and signaled me to get in. "You can drive her, if you would like."

I just stared. "As big a snob as you have always been, I don't get it—you in this car?"

"And what is wrong with it?" he remarked defensively. "This car represents the brainchild of one of this country's great business minds: the car that would save the Chrysler auto company. I drive it as a statement on the ingenuity of capitalism. It should be in a museum."

"That would be better than the road."

"Well, it beats walking."

"Not by much."

"Oh, stop being so Boston. You haven't lived there long enough to become a member of the Volvo-driving, liberal elite."

I stepped up to the car to get a closer look. "What happened to the roof?"

"The roof?"

"Yeah, it's all caved in," I said, pointing to the scraped and mangled metal.

"Paisano."

"Paisano?"

"Yeah, Paisano. It's a light Chianti."

"I know what it is. But a bottle of Chianti made that crater? It must have fallen from a plane."

"No, it was two bottles . . . and my Arizona brothers who drank them."

"I don't know your Arizona brothers. I didn't know you had any brothers at all."

"I don't. They aren't my brothers. They aren't really brothers at all, or at least not to each other. They're these two guys I know from Arizona. Great guys, you know. I call them *my* Arizona brothers because I own them on the basketball court. Everybody else calls them that because they are always together."

"And from Arizona?"

"Of course. You will meet them tonight."

"So, how did they destroy your roof?" I got in the driver's side and held out my hand for the keys.

"No keys," he said. "I accidentally broke a key off in the ignition. All you have to do is turn it."

So I turned the keyless ignition, and to my surprise, it started with a grinding cough, followed by a strong smell of gasoline. I imagined there must be a leak. Then I noticed the dashboard had been gutted and replaced with a TV, facing up at the windshield.

"What the hell is that?"

"A few minor adjustments the Arizona brothers helped me with. We tore out the instrument panel and moved it to the passenger side."

Sure enough, farther off to the right were the speedometer, odometer, and all the additional car gadgets.

"We put in the monitor and hooked it up to a VCR," he said, indicating the place where the radio should have been. There was a VCR interface.

"But the TV is facing up. How do you see it?" I asked. This seemed an obvious problem with the design. I hadn't yet considered the more pertinent question: Why the hell put a TV in the dashboard of the car?

"No, no, no. You see, it's a heads-up display." He hit the play switch and the MGM lion appeared in the windshield. "The monitor is at an angle that casts the image onto the windshield so that you can watch the movie while driving."

"Why would you do that?"

"For long trips, of course. We put this camera in here above you, aimed at the instruments in front of the passenger, so if you want to see them, you hit this toggle and," Milton flipped a switch between the seats and the MGM lion was replaced on the windshield with a projected image of the instrument panel. He smiled broadly. "Heads-up instrumentation—like on those new jet fighters the Air Force is paying millions to build. And we did it with pawnshop equipment and a video-conferencing camera stolen from the business school at Tulane. They are overly reliant upon technology anyway."

"And this is legal?"

"Well, I don't know. The Air Force does it, so it probably isn't."

I didn't want to hear any more about the dashboard.

"So, how did they destroy the roof?" I was stalling for time, hoping the car might die before Milton finished talking.

"Depends who you ask. One said that they went off the road and rolled the car over. But I don't believe him."

"What did the other say?"

"They went off the road and hit someone's balcony, dropping all the furniture and a barbecue pit on the roof of the car."

"Hit a balcony?"

"I presume he meant they hit the supporting columns."

"And you believe that story?"

"Well, there was a large barbecue fork in the car that had apparently gone through the windshield, or else it was already in the car. It is the only bit of evidence, and it supports the balcony story."

"Apart from the overall smashed up condition of the vehicle."

"Well, yes, something happened. But it's cool because they paid to get the windshield fixed."

"And the rest of it?"

"Well, I won it from them in a bet, so I couldn't really ask them to fix it all up."

"So they were driving it after you won it from them?"

"Yes."

"Dare I ask why you let two pseudo brothers from Arizona drive your car on two bottles of Paisano?"

"Well, how else are they going to get around if I don't let them use it? Anyway, I don't drive it all the time. Usually, I rent something for the weekends. For about fifty dollars you can get a convertible or one of those four-wheel drive station wagons. The girls love those things."

8

"GIRLS? EXACTLY HOW old are we talking about?"

"Now, Tim, don't get uppity with me. I prefer a younger crowd. They aren't so commitment oriented. Anyway, the older ones couldn't care less what I drive, and frankly, I prefer a woman who is a little more discriminating."

"I would rather not know what you mean by discriminating, but come on, fifty dollars a weekend? You must be doing pretty well yourself."

"What, haven't you heard?"

"Heard?"

"Nobody told you?" Milton asked, this time drawing two cigars from his coat pocket. "I thought you were on our mailing list."

"Tell me what, for Christ's sake?"

"I am a self-made man," he said, handing me a cigar. He rolled down his window, bit the end from his cigar, and spit it onto the sidewalk.

"What do you mean 'self-made'?" I said and spit the end of my cigar out the window with all the flourish I could manage.

"That's right, self-made and independently wealthy. A modern member of the leisure class." Milton reached under his seat and began feeling around.

I was impressed, but I was skeptical, "And how, exactly, have you made yourself?"

"Credit, of course."

I didn't understand, and so I didn't respond. Milton sensed my confusion.

"You don't get it, do you?" From under his seat, he produced an electric firelighter, the long kind used to ignite barbecue grills.

"No, and I am not sure that I want to get it, whatever it is. It sounds horrible."

"On the contrary, it is splendid. Don't you see?" Milton lit his cigar with a long flame that threatened to singe his eyebrows and then tossed the lighter into my lap. "Let me give you an example of how it works. When you go to pay a restaurant bill and you don't have any cash, you pay with a credit card, right?"

"Uh huh," failing to conceal the lack of interest in my voice.

"Well, I don't ever have any cash. In fact, I don't have any money at all, so I always pay with a credit card."

It was the stupidest thing I had heard in my life. "That sounds brilliant." I pushed the switch on the lighter and braced myself as I ignited my own cigar. "Only, I wonder, Milton, what do you do when you get the credit card bills?"

"Oh please, I have a desk drawer full of those credit card checks. You know, the ones they are always sending you. Hell, they even encourage you to pay off your other cards with them. So I do. And you know what it's like being a graduate student, you get a new, preapproved card in the mail every day and usually with a stack of those checks."

"You're still in school?"

"Of course. How else could I pay my rent?"

"Credit?"

"My landlord is somewhat old-fashioned—won't take those credit card checks, says they are hard to cash. I pay my dissertation fees, collect my graduate stipend, and pay my rent with that. My landlord loves it because I pay him in six-month installments."

"But what about school?"

"What do you mean?"

"I mean, are you still attending classes, are you writing a dissertation? They won't let you stick around indefinitely, will they?"

"Oh no, not indefinitely. And yes, technically, I am writing my dissertation. Of course, I haven't written a word and have absolutely no intention of doing so."

"How long will they let you ride like this?" I handed him back the lighter, and he slid it under his seat.

"Well, that's a good question, and I suppose it depends on how I play it. There is a fellow over in the political science department who spent some time reading everything he could about the Vietnam War and its effects on elections in the '70s. Now he teaches a class on the subject every term—the class is a huge hit. He hasn't written a word on his thesis in years, but the department has no intention of sacking him. They need him to teach the Vietnam course."

"What are you teaching?"

"Oh, nothing special, some introduction to philosophy class. No, I am taking a slightly different approach—the stealth scholar." I nodded, feigning appreciation. "You see, if people never see you around, they assume you are hard at work. So, I never show up at the department. I never attend any of the department functions. I am the department recluse—locked away with my books."

"I don't remember any functions."

"Dreadful affairs, I assure you, though there are a few who recognize a good Scotch and might occasionally bring a bottle, but I never attend anymore. No, the key is to strike the figure of an absent and thoroughly annoyed scholar. I always answer the phone in an angry tone, to remind them that they are disturbing my contemplation. They are all annoying folks themselves and therefore respect this feature in others as a sign of intelligence," he paused and gave me a grin. I didn't need his pause. I understood his poorly crafted doublespeak entirely and figured that his lack of confidence in his listener stemmed from his keeping the company of adolescent women. "Anyway, they more or less leave me be. Of course, it can't go on forever, unless I too can find the philosophical equivalent of the Vietnam War."

Milton's woolly approach to conversation was not unfamiliar to me. When we were roommates studying philosophy at Tulane, I had always marveled at his capacity to turn an idea inside out. It was this ability that made him a remarkable student and challenging raconteur.

"May I use the lighter again?" I asked, and Milton obliged. I hadn't smoked a cigar since graduate school and from a lack of practice had allowed it to burn out. As I held it before the flame, memories from our years at Tulane resurfaced. Those were the gravy days. We had both studied some, of course, but our time was mostly dedicated to diverting ourselves—and we had found a wide variety of diversions. The city had been our oyster, but it was the apartment itself around which our lives had revolved: long dinner parties with other students arguing the finer points of Aristotle until late in the evening, later nights drinking Scotch and watching documentaries about termites in Africa, and early morning basketball before the New Orleans sun transformed the pavement into a skillet. We had installed a basketball net in the driveway behind our apartment that was on the corner of Nashville Avenue and Waters Street. Although he had not started playing until grad school, Milton discovered he had a rare talent. He didn't miss, or at least not very often. Basketball, dinner parties, and late-night binges kept us pretty busy.

When things got dull, we could always count on the appearance of guests to spice things up. As Milton was not from New Orleans and had lived a rather nomadic American childhood, his friends from all over the States would pop in for all sorts of occasions. Mardi Gras and the jazz festival always brought a crowd, but many would come at other times just because it was New Orleans. In between these activities, he and I might find time to attend a class or two each semester. Through it all, we complained bitterly the way all graduate students do: too much work, not enough money, what to do if we graduated. You never appreciate the gravy days until they are gone.

Being back now, it was hard not to miss them and hard not to think about what else I might have missed. When I decided to leave school and seek gainful employment with my uncle, the university graciously offered me a master's degree for my efforts. But after three years in Boston, I had come to the conclusion that work is overrated—yet, per the American way, it allowed me to accumulate a sufficient number of financial obligations to keep working. It was a vicious cycle, and it killed me that Milton had successfully avoided it and milked the system for seven years now, without producing a damn thing. And here the great man sat, in a beat-up car parked on St. Charles Avenue, smoking a fat cigar and looking perfectly satisfied with himself.

"What will you do if someone at the university gives you a time line for completing your degree?" I asked in an effort to assuage my own jealousy.

"Oh, don't start with me. You sound like my parents, for Christ's sake. I am in the middle of my life's work. I can't be bothered with the department's timetables for graduation or society's desire to see us fritter our lives away in some mindless occupation. The revolution is too large to set aside for such petty concerns."

"The revolution?"

"Of course."

"Pray tell."

"Well, you know I have always been a revolutionary."

"I know you used to wear your hair like one of the goddamned Beatles and were always talking nonsense."

"The Beatles? Oh please. I can't stand The Beatles. And, anyway, what do the British know of revolution? They epitomize conservation of the establishment."

"I presume you refer to the common Englishman's ambivalence over the French Revolution?"

"Precisely. They haven't had any real change since 1066, and it took a boatload of Frenchmen with lances to make it happen."

"The French victory at the Battle of Hastings is wrongly seen as marking the ascendancy of the cavalry in European warfare," I said, hoping to derail his pontifications.

"William the Conqueror borrowed money from Jewish bankers to finance his invasion of England, marking the ascendancy of derivative swapping and high finance," Milton answered proudly, having obviously given this a great deal of thought.

"And this interpretation of history transformed you into a revolutionary?"

"You recall the bomb scare in Gibson Hall?" Milton said, blowing a prodigious cloud of smoke out the window.

"You mean when you set off all the smoke bombs in the air-conditioning ducts?"

"That was my first planned action against the establishment," he said proudly.

"It did spare me a three-hour lecture on Wittgenstein. So, what's with the new haircut?" I asked, referring to his tidy Ivy League coiffure. "Hardly revolutionary."

"Well, I am no longer into smoke bombs," he said, stroking his massive head while looking in the vanity mirror attached to the sun visor. "I have devised a new plan for bringing the capitalist economy in this country to its knees. My new look reflects my new revolutionary tactics."

"Why?"

"What?"

"Why bring capitalism to its knees?"

"Well, for nothing better to do, I suppose. Do I really need a reason?"

"You aren't working then?"

"Heavens, no. You know, I never really took to it, work that is. And what is the point anyway? By working you do nothing but contribute to capital."

"So you're a Marxist?"

"In a manner of speaking, yes, but with the collapse of the Soviet Union, I have come to the conclusion that Marx misunderstood the manner in which capitalism must be deposed."

"Go on," I said.

"The weakness of capital is credit." As he spoke, I stared out the window through the heads-up display of the dashboard. "You see, most of the money in the country is made by giving out credit and then charging interest on that credit, right?"

"OK." I wasn't convinced. Hadn't Marx argued that wealth was made by the exploitation of labor?

"You don't follow me?"

"I do." I didn't, but I could see that an explanation was coming and asking for one was unnecessary.

"Mortgages, stocks, bonds, government loans," Milton waved his hand as if this list were endless, "it is all credit. And those loans sponsor all manner of economic activity, public and private."

"OK," I repeated, starting to understand his point.

"So what happens if our national debt, public and private, gets so big that all the debtors must default on their loans?"

"Well, the country would go belly-up, I guess."

"And that would be the end of capitalism. The monetary system would fail entirely, and when the U.S. economy goes south, every other industrial nation in the world will follow her down. Money will be useless, because money is a form of credit. So the world will return to a more natural system of barter, in which each individual maintains a more authentic relationship to what he, or she, produces."

I nodded. "So you believe that the government will default on the national debt?"

"Unfortunately, no. While things looked promising in the mid-'80s with Reagan running up the largest debt in the history of the world, any hope for that seems to have faded. All these damned balanced budget people! Don't they see that the better the economy is, the more the people suffer? Reagan was a genius, a visionary. Spend every penny on the military, which has no real value, and ultimately bankrupt the nation. Reagan was a closet anarchist. Down with capitalism!" Milton shouted into the warm evening air. "But Washington won't stay the course. Sure, the government spends money like a teenage girl at the mall with her parents' credit card, but the Chinese possess an endless willingness to buy U.S. bonds and buoy the U.S. economy." He paused and took a deep breath. "No, it is going to require the private citizens of this country to step up and default."

"You don't think that you will be able to run up a large enough debt on your own to default the federal treasury?"

"No, of course not. That is why it will take a revolution. We must rise up against the establishment, set an example, and encourage everyone to run all their credit cards to the max. They can even pay their taxes on credit. Isn't it beautiful? A revolutionary strategy that plays upon America's greatest strength: mindless consumerism. Eventually, the private debt becomes so great it is unpayable. The entire nation brought to its knees in one cunning stroke."

"And you are leading this revolution?"

"Yes. But we aren't going anywhere."

"The revolution?"

"No, the car." Distracted by our conversation and reluctant to pilot Milton's renovated K-car, I had not moved us from our parking spot in front of The Columns Hotel.

"Do you want me to drive?" he asked.

"Please." Thank God, I was thinking. This vehicle was an accident waiting to happen. The proof was that at least one accident had happened already.

Milton slid his massive frame over mine as we traded seats in a maneuver that would have made a splendid shot for the Mapplethorpe collection. He put the car in gear, as indicated by the windshield display, and took off uptown on St. Charles Avenue. The Mermaid was in the Warehouse District. We were heading the opposite direction.

"Aren't we going the wrong way?" I started to ask but then let it go. What difference did it make where we went? He probably couldn't see through the heads-up display anyway. I changed the subject. "And the Arizona brothers, what do they do?"

"Mostly play basketball. Of course, they drink too."

"I mean for a living."

"Oh, I don't know. But they don't work, if that is what you mean."

That was precisely what I meant. "I suppose they are your disciples."

"Oh no, they were doing fine before they ever met me."

"How was that?"

"That I met them or that they were doing fine?"

"How did you meet them?" I clarified.

"Playing basketball. We met at the courts on Magazine Street, and I asked them to move in with me."

"After a few shots you ask some strangers from Arizona to move in with you?" Milton had never been a Good Samaritan, so I suspected there was something less than benevolence involved here.

"Something like that. Actually, they were living out of their car, so when I won it from them, they needed a place to stay. I needed a roommate, or two, to help with the rent, so it was a perfect fit."

"And how did you win the car?"

"Twenty-one. They are both really good, but they play that West Coast basketball. They are too soft under the basket, and they don't play with the three free throws rule."

Milton rarely missed free throws. When playing twenty-one with Milton, you had to limit the number of free throws a player gets after making a shot. Typically, the rules of twenty-one allow a player to shoot until he misses, but the three free throws rule requires that after three consecutive free throws, the player must put the ball back into play. I could imagine that without this rule, Milton would have disposed of them quickly.

"So you got the car, and they got a place to live."

"Yeah, basketball's been *beery, beery* good to me," he said with a smile, before turning serious. "But we have a problem that basketball can't fix."

"Your dates?"

"Yeah. Have you got a couple dollars?"

"Wait, tell me about these dates."

"It's really nothing. I simply have, well, two girlfriends."

"Two?"

"Yes," he paused, "it isn't as bad as it sounds. You see, one lives in Baton Rouge and the other lives in Oxford."

"England?"

"Mississippi."

"England would have made it easier to understand."

"They don't know about one another. I guess that is obvious," he admitted, chuckling. "The unpleasant part is that they both chose this weekend to come visit."

"You?"

"Well, yes, but they are not staying with me. They are both from New Orleans and staying with their families for the weekend." He paused to get his intellectual bearings. "It's merely a problem of Friday night logistics and feminine sentimentality. Both girls expect me to entertain them this evening. To paraphrase The Beach Boys, you cannot leave your best girl home on a Friday night. Nobody is more keenly aware of that than the out-of-town girlfriend."

"And you want me to break the news to one of them for you and comfort her after you've explained that you've been lying for God knows how long?"

"No, no, no, nothing like that at all. Are you kidding? I have no intention of breaking it off with either of them. You see, that is where you come in."

"I am afraid I don't see it at all."

"Well, obviously, neither girl has met the other or knows anything at all about the other. Now, they both believe they are going on a date with me tonight. How that happened I cannot explain, but I blame it on one of the Arizona brothers forgetting to give me a message until this morning. Anyway, it's quite simple. We just pick the girls up, each girl thinks she is on a date with me and that the other is with you."

"Pardon?" I was sure I missed something.

"Yeah, just like that."

"Like what?" I must have missed something.

"I just tell both girls that we are double-dating. Each will naturally imagine the other girl is with you."

"Nice try, but it won't work."

Milton turned right onto Carrollton Avenue where St. Charles and Carrollton intersect and nearly hit a black sedan failing to yield on a left turn. Milton never saw the sedan and never slowed down. The sedan was forced to lock up its brakes in order to avoid hitting us. Apparently, this angered the driver deeply. The sedan swerved around us and illustrated its horn in an unfriendly fashion. Milton leaned over me and tossed his cigar into the window of the vehicle as it rapidly passed us on the right, narrowly avoiding the parked cars, all while the driver made hand gestures at us. It was hard to see exactly what these gestures were before the sedan sped away.

My vision was obscured by the K-car's heads-up display.

9

MILTON PRODUCED A FRESH CIGAR from his jacket pocket, looked at me, and asked for a light. I found the electric lighter and passed it to him. Milton was able to operate it while driving, and soon clouds of smoke were once again billowing from the driver's-side window. He smiled his effusive smile and spoke as if addressing an audience.

"Have a little faith in human nature." The black sedan was now only distant taillights hurtling down Carrollton.

"This double date idea is hardly natural."

"Nothing is more natural than vanity," he asserted.

I had no idea how this comment supported his rapidly flagging argument. Rather than bang my brains mercilessly against the Möbius strip that was Milton's thought process, I chose a less theoretical approach.

"So what do we do when both girls try to get into the front seat with Dr. Love?"

"Oh, that's easy. From the look on your face, I thought you had a legitimate concern. We explain that you sprained a hamstring playing basketball and must sit in the front seat so that you can stretch out your leg.

These K-cars have no backseat legroom. Anyway, that means both girls must sit in the back."

I thought he must be insane. "You're insane."

"But you know it will work."

"Until we get out of the car. Where are we going anyway? I mean, where are you going, because I am not going on this deranged double date."

"I already told you. We are going to The Mermaid. That all-girl band is playing."

"I forgot. They are awful."

"Never mind the band. You just pay attention to our dates."

"Which one?" I smirked.

"This is a piece of cake. The Mermaid will be packed with folks we know. We just send the women for beer and then disappear in the crowd. We mingle."

"You are perfectly insane." I had proof now.

"But it will work. Anyway, you've always been good luck. I couldn't ask for a better accomplice."

"Don't count on my luck. It ran dry years ago."

"What? Mr. Lucky? Gone? Say it isn't so."

"Sorry. And as for your scheme, it won't work, and I won't do it," but Milton wasn't listening.

"Did you say you had more money?" he asked, pulling into a K&B.

What did Milton need from a drugstore? Then it dawned on me. "I am not buying you condoms."

He ignored me. "A jug of Paisano, if you please. I would get it myself, but they won't take my credit cards anymore."

"And I wonder why that is," I asked, mostly to myself, but did his bidding anyway. I stepped into the K&B and stepped out four dollars poorer but sporting a handsome jug of wine. I stuck my head into the window of the K-car. "Have you got glasses?"

"Glasses? For Paisano?"

I walked back into the K&B, bought a pack of eight wineglasses for five dollars, and returned to Milton. "I am too old to drink cheap wine from a jug."

"It doesn't taste any better from a glass."

"Yeah, well, it feels better against my lips, and at my age that is worth something."

"I knew you were a romantic," Milton laughed and pulled out in front of another car that seemed to be coming fast. He gunned it. The gunning it was only recognizable from the sound the engine made and not from any great acceleration. In fact, the automatic transmission of the K-car seemed a bit stymied by his enthusiasm and bounced around between first and second gear for about thirty seconds. Milton spoke over the sound of the other car's horn. "Holly is staying with her folks on Audubon Boulevard, just off Fontainebleau. We will pick her up first."

I opened the bottle of wine and the box of glasses. Despite the car's leaping about over the broken street, I was able to fill one glass and drink it before we reached the light at Claiborne Avenue. I started a second before the light turned green. The intersection between Carrollton Avenue and Claiborne was the end of the streetcar line and, in my opinion, marked the end of uptown. Technically, uptown extended north all the way to Interstate 10, but as far as I was concerned, Claiborne was the dividing line. Of course, most people didn't care very much about what counted as uptown, downtown, midtown, Lakeview, and so on. For most people, these were just names. But for me, uptown was a way of life. Uptown was slowed by narrow streets, cooled under broad oaks, illuminated by Loyola and Tulane, and serenaded to sleep at night by the horns of the great ships on the river. This was uptown, and it had nothing to do with the hustle and bustle of the four-lane Claiborne Avenue, lined with all manner of modern commerce: banks, gas stations, grocery stores, and strip malls. I had grown up uptown, had attended college uptown, and had always steered clear of the rest of the city as much as possible.

In my experience, I had found it was always a mistake to leave uptown. And although Holly's parents technically lived uptown, our final destination, The Mermaid, was definitely not. Uptown New Orleans is a sleepy little sanctuary nestled precariously in the midst of one of America's great urban experiments—an experiment that I felt was never completely comfortable with itself. I had always hated cities, even the beautiful ones. Philadelphia, San Francisco, Boston, New York, they are all magnificent, but they are cold and hard, with few soft spots where you can stop and rest. In uptown New Orleans, you can rest. As bad as my first day back had been, returning to uptown restored a certain peace in my life that was missing in Boston. It was for the sake of that peace that I felt some apprehension about crossing Claiborne.

Milton accelerated at the green. The car lurched over a great crater in the intersection and the remainder of my Paisano landed on my slacks. "Damn these roads. This whole city should be condemned."

"It was condemned, many times. But what are folks to do? Move to Jefferson Parish?" Milton winced at the idea. "Anyway, that's why I drink from the bottle. I think it was drinking out of glasses that got the Arizona brothers into trouble. They are accustomed to those baby-bottomed Arizona highways. These goat trails overwhelmed them." He reached for the jug, but I pulled it away. I was riding in a fake car—a K-car that looked like it had fallen from a bridge—drinking fake wine, on my way to pick up my fake date. I was not going to allow any further affront to my dignity by having Milton slurp wine from the jug in front of me. I poured him a glass, trying carefully not to spill it, and offered it to him.

"My God, you're drunk," he said, looking me in the eye and taking the weaving glass from my hand.

"Not drunk enough. Not drunk enough for this escapade." Of course, I was precisely drunk enough. Conscious of my drunkenness, I was able to ignore my common sense telling me to get out and walk home. "How else could you have talked me into this insanity?"

"I didn't."

"That's what I mean." I realized the Paisano was having a more disabling impact on my speech and coordination than the bourbon. Perhaps the bourbon was only now really kicking in?

"What were you doing at The Columns?" Milton asked, somehow reading my mind.

"I was with Jane."

"Jane?"

"Yeah, it was kind of a date."

"It didn't look like a date to me. You were by yourself."

"She left mad."

"Mad, huh? What did you say?"

"I don't remember."

"Oh, that's what you said?"

"What?" He was confusing me again.

"I know you," Milton returned his empty glass for a refill and turned right at Fontainebleau. "I know both of you. You are both afraid to say anything. You could probably make love to her and not say anything."

He reflected a moment.

"She has been in love with you ever since I have known her and God only knows how long before that."

I poured the wine.

"Why she's ever loved you, I cannot guess, but it was always clear that you felt the same way. Everyone knew it. Even your girlfriends knew it. That's why they were always pissed off at you."

Milton took the wineglass from me.

"Why do you love her?" he asked.

I shrugged. I wasn't sure myself. Does anyone ever really know?

10

"I KNOW WHAT YOU SAID," Milton announced, interrupting my thoughts.

"You got her all worked up and then you said nothing. You are both the same, you know, the same personality. The only difference is that it is more becoming on a woman." Milton drank his wine. "You two might as well be the same person. I would have made love to Jane myself, except that it would have been like sleeping with you. Thanks," he said, handing me his wineglass again. "I can't believe that after all these years you still have a thing for her."

"It's confusing," I admitted, topping off his glass and giving it back.

"So, did she say anything? Did she finally break the silence?"

"Yeah, she said she's planning to marry my brother."

The comment wasn't intended to be funny, but most of the wine in Milton's mouth ended up on the windshield, which served to clean it a bit. The rest went on his pants. He didn't seem to notice. Milton was laughing hysterically.

"Sweet Jesus!" He stopped the car abruptly in the middle of Fontainebleau. "Your brother?"

"Yeah," I took advantage of the pause and replenished his glass. "It gets worse."

"Worse?" Someone behind us honked. Milton unconsciously gave them the finger so as not to interrupt his thought. "How could it get worse, unless—"

"We are in the middle of the road," I reminded him.

"—she's pregnant," he said and hit the gas. The car responded in its resentful fashion, but the horns behind us subsided.

"Yeah."

"No."

"Yeah, she's really pregnant."

"No."

"Yeah," I repeated, tiring of this game.

"And you?"

"No, I am not pregnant."

He relaxed and turned to me.

"This is rich." He paused. "What did you do? Did you panic? I would have panicked. That's the sensible thing to do, isn't it?"

"Yeah, I guess I did." My date with Jane was supposed to be a reunion, interesting and mildly provocative. Instead, it had been a disaster. I panicked.

Milton turned an abrupt right onto Audubon Boulevard and pulled over. "So, when is the date?"

"Which one?"

"Both, I guess."

"I don't know, but I must imagine soon, right? The baby can't be more than nine months away. That means they have to get married before then. They haven't officially told anyone yet, but they are planning to announce their engagement tomorrow night at my sister's debutante ball."

"Oh no, at the ball?"

"Yeah."

"How tacky."

"It was my brother's idea."

"Naturally. Beneath that new veneer of sophistication remains a significant degree of commonness. What about Jane?"

"I think she plans to be drunk for the whole thing."

"The marriage?" He grinned.

"Well, at least during the announcement of their engagement."

"What do you intend to do?"

"What can I do, except hand them the rings?"

"Rings?"

"Yeah, my brother asked me to be his best man."

"Does it never end?" Milton was clearly enjoying this. He had a great penchant for creating drama, but created drama cannot contend with the real thing.

"I am beginning to think it was a bad idea to visit."

I hated drama. I preferred a neat, organized procession of events that was neither dull nor upsetting. Milton's passion for drama intrigued me, but I never really wished to be the source of his pleasure.

"Are you kidding? I can't believe I let you go to Boston. You're so amusing."

He drank the wine and passed me back the glass. He was beaming and scheming. I could see the Machiavellian gleam in his eyes. He was trying to insert himself into the drama. He was a thrill seeker.

"You've got to do something."

Here it comes, I thought to myself.

"You've got to stop her! You can't just sit there and be party to that stiff stealing the woman you've spent your whole life pining for."

"You shouldn't end a sentence with a preposition."

"And you shouldn't let your brother marry the love of your life while you watch."

"Love of my life?" Milton certainly had a way of getting to the heart of the matter. I wasn't convinced that Jane was the love of my life. I wasn't sure who would fit that category if required to identify that person.

"It sounds better that way." Milton was stoking the drama. "Anyway, you can't let him announce their engagement at the ball. It will totally destroy the atmosphere and utterly ruin my chances."

"For what?" I asked, but before he could answer, I added, "What's it got to do with you, and why are you even going to be there?"

I wasn't angry. I was relieved to know that somebody else found this whole thing appalling. Being appalled didn't require love; it only required common sense. Anyone would find this engagement appalling.

"Of course I will be there. I attend all the major debutante balls in the city. In fact, I believe that I remain uptown's most eligible bachelor. My newfound wealth—"

"You mean credit," I inserted.

"Yes, well, it is the same thing. Anyway, my newfound credit has made me the darling of the New Orleans social scene. I am always invited to these events, and I happen to have my eye on one debutante in particular this season. She will be at the ball tomorrow."

Milton, a debutante aficionado? This was new and nearly as absurd as this double date upon which we were preparing to embark. The double date was ridiculous, but it was a useful diversion from the less pleasant topic of William and Jane. I indulged myself.

"What about your girlfriends?" I asked the obvious question.

"I did not invite them, if that is what you mean. I should imagine they will be busy with their families. One of them has a debutante ball of her own to attend, but I have begged out of it on account of a very sick aunt."

"I assume there is no sick aunt."

Of course I knew the answer, but it was part of our banter. Milton always made absurd claims, claims that begged to be questioned, and would then offer the thinnest explanation imaginable, an explanation that could not possibly pose as an explanation at all. Somehow, this was the key to his sincerity, that his lies were always utterly unmasked.

"I am confident that there is a sick aunt somewhere, and I see no reason that she should suffer in vain."

I obliged him. "How thoughtful of you."

"And with the excuse in place, I shall be free to work the ball."

Milton turned to me and grimaced. "Unfortunately, once your brother makes his silly announcement, all the place will be abuzz with it, and the girls will gather and talk of nothing but weddings. In other words, a total disaster for the bachelors."

"It could be no more a disaster than normal. Those balls are always unbearably tedious."

"On the contrary," he insisted, "they are wonderful, if you know how to play them. But once the conversation turns to weddings, well, the girls lose that sense of free-spiritedness and start casting about for husbands."

"Husbands?" I asked.

"Yes, precisely. They ask you what you do for a living. That's splendid news for your medical students, law students, even a business major might stand a chance, if he can convince the girl he is destined to inherit his father's company. But a post-Cold War Marxist like me is screwed. No, we must not allow this announcement. It would ruin everything."

I contemplated his concern. "You're pursuing a debutante?"

"Yes."

"But they are so young. Not one can be over twenty."

"Oh no. Most are not nearly twenty. I think eighteen is more common."

"Lovely."

"Now don't get all snotty with me or our dates," he defended.

"Why would I get snotty with them?"

"Well," anxiously, "they are both freshmen in college."

"Freshmen?"

"OK. Freshwomen, if you prefer."

"I prefer them older."

I poured myself another glass of Paisano and took a deep breath. It seemed that Milton had gone from eccentric philosophy student to cad, child-molesting cad, child-molesting cad with bad credit, and he was dragging me in with him. How had it happened?

"How do you meet these girls?"

"At debutante parties mostly, but there are plenty of high society parties year-round, hosted by rich old farts sporting their freshly bloomed daughters. They practically beg you to date their daughters. One old man even gave me his daughter's number after I met him on the golf course."

"Did you call her?"

"We are picking her up right now." Milton pointed to the house on the right. I began to feel dizzy, queasy. I handed Milton the bottle of wine. He poured himself a glass, drank it, and turned to me. "Don't forget about the knee injury: right leg, basketball, can't bend it."

"I thought you said hamstring?"

"Please keep it straight. I'll be right back." Milton slipped his heavy frame out of the car.

I swallowed my wine and closed my eyes. I knew this could only end in disaster. Milton's schemes always did.

Holly was beautiful. Of course she was beautiful. In a sweater, short skirt, and tights, she was everything a girl could be at eighteen, without everything she might be at thirty. Not that I disliked women my own age. I preferred them. Jane was thirty. But they rarely came without physical or emotional baggage. At eighteen, a girl still has that new car smell.

I noticed her skin first—smooth, porcelain, radiant even at night—then her breasts, which seemed to levitate, reaching for the stars. I am a realist by nature and feared that this spell she cast by walking from her door to the car would be broken by the first words from her mouth. But she climbed into the backseat and said only, "Hello, Tim, sorry about your ankle."

"Knee," I corrected and suddenly felt like the idiot I expected her to be. She remained quiet as Milton spoke endlessly about my new injury. He had already explained my being the next girl's date but was now trying to preempt all possible questions so that Holly would not ask when girlfriend number two, apparently named Rachel, got into the car.

When he stopped, Holly told me what a pleasant surprise it was to meet me and that she was looking forward to hearing about Boston. She was enchanting.

I didn't know where Rachel lived, but it was on one of those potholed streets in the Garden District, in a big white house with a broad second-story porch supported by Greek columns and shaded by ancient oak trees. I continued to spill wine on myself, now trying to pour a glass for Holly. She accepted the glass with some caution, and we both drank. Milton went in to pick up Rachel. Holly didn't find it odd that Milton was fetching Rachel, and I attributed that to his exegesis on my knee injury. He made it sound like I would be having surgery the following day. I began to wonder what Holly might think when I started walking around The Mermaid. I was not going to limp all night to save Milton's date.

During his absence, Holly remained attentive to my very weak efforts at conversation. "Do you like the wine?"

"It's Paisano," she said flatly.

"Yes."

"No, that was my answer to your question, 'Do I like the wine?'"

"Oh, I see." She was clever. She was eighteen, she was beautiful, and she was clever. I knew girls like that when I was eighteen, but they wouldn't talk to me. They were always dating men ten years older, and it had always pissed me off. Who were those men? Now I knew: They were me, ten years later.

"But I like it anyway, and I appreciate the wineglass. That must have been your idea. Milton usually drinks it out of the bottle. I don't suppose it deserves a glass, but it does improve the overall experience, don't you think?"

I nodded. "Yes, on the lips," pointing to my lips in a way that was a little suggestive but mostly just absurd. Fortunately, Rachel and Milton appeared at that moment, saving me further embarrassment.

Rachel was not unlike Holly, except that she had red, rather than blonde, hair. She was perhaps a bit shorter and heavier—in the right places. Maybe my moral compass had been damaged by the Paisano, but I was feeling steadily less judgmental of Milton's dating practices. Looking at Rachel and Holly left me with a warm feeling inside. Perhaps that, too, was the Paisano.

Rachel accepted a glass of wine, and we were off to the Warehouse District. Milton turned up the volume on the radio to discourage talk.

"Loose lips sink ships," he shouted over the voice of some semipopular, whiny female throwing her romantic disappointment into sharp relief.

The scenery went by in a Paisano blur, but I kept a vigilant watch for empty glasses. Before we had turned onto Annunciation, the jug was empty.

THE MERMAID

Why do people give to beggars and not philosophers?

Athenian Citizen

Because they think they may one day be lame or blind,
but never expect that they will turn to philosophy.

Diogenes of Sinope

Aquavit Rickey

2 OZ AQUAVIT RICKEY
1 TSP KÜMMEL
½ OZ LIME JUICE

Pour into a highball glass with
ice and fill with club soda.

11

THE MERMAID LOOKED EXACTLY as I had left it three years ago. I was drunker now than then, but it was the same. And the neighborhood was the same—the northern corner of the reviving Warehouse District. I call it "reviving" because the revival had begun many years earlier and had still not extended much beyond the southeastern end that nudged up against the French Quarter. The northern portion of the district was still pretty dismal, but it did make a rather appealing post-apocalyptic background for a neo-industrial, urban bar.

The patrons were the same. Milton pulled up onto the sidewalk and stopped the car among those mingling outside the bar. An ungainly mix of Goths, frat boys, and nighttime hippies wearing black accessories to their Costa Rican paraphernalia. Maybe like me they were drunker now too, but they looked the same.

"Hasn't changed much, has it?" I asked Milton.

He turned to me, smiled, and then announced to everyone, "We're here. Tim, do you need help getting out?"

I said, "Thank you, I could use some help," before I realized that he was referring to my knee and not my intoxication. He didn't help me. In fact, he jumped out of the car and shouted at everyone, "I will meet you inside," and disappeared. Both girls got out and, leaving me behind, wandered toward the stage area outside the bar. There was quite a crowd amassed around the stage, watching as someone shouted instructions to the roadies rushing about in an attempt to set things up for the show. I collected the wineglasses and put them back into the cardboard box. I didn't fancy the idea of returning to the car and sitting on one unexpectedly.

The bar was dark, and before my eyes adjusted, I felt someone pressing a glass into my hand. It was Milton. "Guys, this is Tim. Tim, these are the Arizona brothers."

"Hey, we've heard about you," said the slightly shorter, darker of the two in that Southern California accent that pervades Arizona. "You're the guy who was so lucky at the track."

"Oh, yeah. Cool, dude. Those must have been awesome times," said the other one. "How's it going?"

I turned to Milton. "Dude?"

"They're from Arizona," he shrugged. The Arizona brothers didn't seem to fit The Mermaid dress code. Nor, as Milton had half-explained, did they even look to be related. Neither wore black, and one was black. The black one was wearing a pink oxford and khaki pants. The white one was dressed in a blue oxford and white cargo pants. They were both drinking something brown on the rocks. I tasted the drink I was handed. Scotch, expensive Scotch. Not that I had a discerning palate when it came to Scotch, but I could tell by the way the flavor failed to commingle happily with the afterburn of the Paisano that it was not the house brand.

"Crappy," I answered the brothers, "but nice Scotch. A couple of these might change my outlook."

"Milton said you tweaked your knee," said the pink one.

I laughed. "It's not my knee that's the problem."

"It's his love life," Milton said.

"Love?" asked the blue brother.

"He had a date tonight that went south," Milton explained.

"You had a date tonight?" asked the other brother.

"Quick date," added his brother.

"Not a date," I said, adding cleverly, "somewhere between zero and three dates."

They both looked at Milton for help.

"He had a date with Jane. Some girl he has been in love with for years but never done anything about. You know the type. You've been in love with her forever, and everyone knows she is perfect for you. And she digs you, and you are paralyzed to act. That's Jane."

They both laughed, and the pink brother said, "Yeah, sure, everybody has a Jane. Mine was a girl from eleventh grade. Unbelievable girl. Smart. She moved to New York to become an investment banker or something. She's probably on her second husband by now."

The taller, blue brother piped in. "Yeah, my Jane was from the third grade. Amy Hiashi. Japanese girl. Amazing. God knows what happened to her, but I still think about her."

"Can't do much about third grade, can you?" I inserted.

"Not now."

"My Jane was Linda Evangelista," added Milton.

"You met Linda Evangelista?" asked a brother. I couldn't tell which one it was. They sounded the same.

"No, not met, but I knew all I needed to know from the cover of all those women's magazines in the grocery store, but I never did anything about it. Now I have to live with the sorrow of knowing I let my Jane get away."

"Yeah, well, my Jane happens to be the real Jane, who left me at The Columns tonight," as if that trumped their Janes.

"And is having your brother's baby," Milton added. I couldn't believe his lack of discretion.

"Wow," said a brother.

"Bummer, dude," offered the other.

"Thanks, Milton."

"And they are going to announce their engagement tomorrow at Tim's sister's debut," he continued mercilessly.

"Hatin' it," whined a brother. I couldn't tell which.

"And Tim is supposed to be the best man." He wouldn't stop.

"Thank you for making sure everyone in this bar knows that my life is shit," I said to Milton.

"Dude, what are you gonna do?"

"Yeah, you got to do something," the other chimed in. To his brother, he added, "Sucks to be him."

I turned to the taller, whiter brother in blue and said, "I'm afraid I can do nothing except drink your kindly chosen Scotch," and I finished what remained and then placed the empty glass on the bar in a dramatic manner that I hoped would signal the bartender for another.

"Drink up, dude, but I think you ought to do something," said the black and pink brother.

"He must do something, because if he doesn't, the debutante ball will be ruined by this engagement announcement," reminded Milton.

"Totally," said the blue brother, suddenly making the connection. "It will put all the debutantes out of sorts."

"Yeah," said the black brother, "and I'm renting a tux for the occasion."

"These two are going to the ball?" I asked Milton, before I realized what a snob I must have seemed.

"As my guests."

"Guests?"

"I'm always invited to these functions, and I am usually encouraged to bring guests."

I looked at the black and pink brother for a moment and thought of the club where the ball would be held. I had never seen a black person there who wasn't part of the service staff. I knew that in theory the club didn't discriminate, but I also knew that the members were not of a particularly theoretical bent. Still, Milton exuded confidence, and I realized that if he had convinced New Orleans society that he was the most eligible bachelor in town, then he could probably convince them that this pink man was not really black. But perhaps this was just Yankee snobbery I had picked up in Boston. I hated the way the Bostonians I met always spoke of New Orleans as a backwater haven for scandal and discrimination, as if Boston were free of either. Had I become one of those irritating social justice Bostonians? Perhaps this Arizona brother was as welcome at the club as any wealthy individual might be. Certainly the club discriminated against the poor, but that was a form of discrimination that everyone, especially Bostonians, never seemed to mind. If he had money, and Milton would see to it that he projected such an appearance, would he be welcomed with open arms? Probably. I reflected on this a moment, trying to get my mind around the issue—whether discrimination on the basis of wealth was acceptable. Why? Presumably because it is OK to discriminate on the basis of choices people make, and rich people chose to be rich and the poor chose to be poor. But didn't the feminist theorist Judith Butler argue that gender was a performance, which would mean it was chosen, and if chosen, then shouldn't we be able to discriminate on the basis of gender? That didn't seem right, but I couldn't find the error in my logic. Was I missing a step? Nope. Couldn't do it. Too much bourbon, Paisano, and Scotch. My mind wandered from these thoughts back to my companions, who were busy gathering chairs around a table.

My Scotch arrived, and Milton led me to a seat.

"Where are the girls?" I asked. He ignored me.

"We have got to come up with a strategy for derailing the announcement," he said.

"A strategy? Why?"

"Dude, to rescue Jane from this bummer brother."

"And to save what would otherwise be a totally lame party," added the second brother. I drank my Scotch, and everyone followed my lead. Milton gestured toward the bar for another round. I wondered who was paying.

Milton kept the Scotch coming, but it wasn't helping. The brothers were throwing out absurd plans involving kidnapping my brother or drugging him or some other form of violence that would wear off in the morning. Outside, I could hear folks cheering as the band began. They were still terrible. I imagined that Rachel and Holly must be mingling. They were too attractive to get bored in a crowd. Somebody would entertain them. I finished another Scotch and returned to the conversation.

"Roberto will know what to do," said Milton. He shouted at a thin man dressed in black jeans and a magenta, silk button-down. "Roberto, *vieni qui.*"

Roberto turned with a huge smile, said something to a woman whose arm was draped about his shoulder, and walked over to join us.

"Milton, how are you?" he said, trying to overcome a heavy accent. The Arizona brothers grinned with confidence. This was obviously a man for whom they had a great deal of respect.

"We've got a problem, Roberto, a problem that requires your particular skills with women." Milton motioned to the bartender to bring another Scotch and then directed Roberto's attention at me. "The woman he loves is planning to marry his brother."

Roberto shrugged and then took my hand in a way that should have made me uncomfortable, but instead calmed me and cleared away at least a small portion of the damage the alcohol had done. "You love this woman, no?"

I said nothing, just stared at my hand in his.

"You take her hand, and you hold it, like this. You tell her, her skin is very beautiful."

"Actually, Roberto, the problem is not of that nature," interrupted Milton. "It isn't really a seduction technique that we need. In fact, we are working under the assumption that this woman already likes Tim more than the emetic fiancé brother."

"I am sorry. I do not understand the problem," Roberto said in an irritated voice and reached for the glass of Scotch being delivered to the table.

"She's pregnant with my brother's baby, OK," I said, frustrated now that I had become the center of this absurd conspiracy. "It's hopeless. There is nothing I can do except sit back and watch."

"I still don't understand. You say that you love this woman?"

"Yes," I said, less out of conviction than anger.

"Did you tell her?"

"How could I? She is carrying my brother's baby. What am I to say? 'I love you, Jane. Marry me, Jane. We'll raise my brother's baby in Bostonian bliss, Jane.'"

"I don't know about this Bostonian bliss thing, but yes to everything else."

"Do you know the word 'baby' in English?" I asked him, no longer concealing my growing ire. "*Bambino* or *bambina*," I said very slowly, trying to enunciate the Italian clearly. Roberto gave Milton a curious look and then turned back to me. I tried another approach.

"Do you understand how this works? My family wouldn't allow such a thing. They will do the limbo just to cover up the soon-to-be-obvious fact that Jane and

William conceived this child before they were married. They would have to be yoga masters to cope with the social distortions created by my running off with Jane."

"I am afraid my English is not that good," he said at the end of my tirade and turned to Milton. "What does he mean 'do this Limbo'? Nobody with sense wants to be in Limbo."

"He means that his family is proper and upstanding. They cannot countenance such an unseemly social maneuver. The kid's father would become the uncle, and the uncle would become the father—much too messy for the Schmidts."

It was not at all clear that Roberto understood the problem, but he nodded and decided to start again.

"I am not precisely sure I understand this American maneuver," he said, glancing over at the woman he had just left and beaming a rakish smile at her, "but I think people in America are not so different from people in Italy." Roberto turned back to address me. "So the families must not be so different either."

I turned to Milton. "He doesn't know my family."

The Italian continued unfazed. "If you are in love with her, you have no choice, you must tell her. This is not Italian or American. This is universal."

Everyone nodded in agreement, and the pink brother slapped Roberto across the back to show his appreciation.

Tell her the truth, they were all saying, acting as if the problem had been solved. Milton called for another round of drinks. I got up to find the bathroom.

12

THE ALL-GIRL BAND was going full swing now, their militant chords infiltrating the building and abusing even those who had attempted to hide at the bar. The sound was somewhat muffled in the back, near the bathrooms, which may have accounted for the crowd gathered there. The number of bodies created a defensive ring blocking the restroom entrance, and penetrating that barrier was proving quite a challenge. With a bit too much enthusiasm, I nudged past two art-deco type girls, lost my footing, and stumbled into the back of another girl entertaining three men. I bumped her slightly harder than what could be forgiven with an "excuse me," and one of the fellows stepped forward to teach me some manners. The guy wasn't as big as a refrigerator, but he was certainly beyond what I considered my "weight class." I didn't get much of a chance to say anything before he had grabbed me by my collar and dragged me toward him. I tried to remember what Bruce Lee did in situations like this, but the image wasn't materializing. Instead, I could only recall Milton telling me many years ago that most bar fights start near the bathroom. This line of thinking was not particularly useful in my current predicament. The fellow pulled me in close, so we were chin to chin, and I noticed, with some displeasure, that he was not only large but also handsome. That was the worst blow. While I didn't mind being beaten by an ugly brute, this guy was more of the *GQ* type—big but still quite the cover boy. There could be no honor in being pummeled by this ape-sized George Clooney. At that moment, I heard the girl pipe up behind me.

"Josh, let him go. He's a friend of mine."

It was Holly. She pulled me away from Josh.

"It's no big deal—he just bumped into me," she lectured him, before turning to me. "Are you OK?"

I wasn't. I felt rather rattled. I said yes.

I stepped into the restroom and threw up in the sink. It was a deep, purging expulsion that relieved me of the Scotch and the better part of the Paisano I had consumed in Milton's K-car. I was still drunk, but in the absence of the Scotch, my vision began to clear. I washed my face in the sink that now smelled of Scotch and Paisano, rearranged my clothes, and took a deep breath. I didn't fancy walking back into the bar past Josh and his buddies, but I couldn't recall if there was another way out. If I could exit through the back, I could walk around the bar and return to Milton and the Arizona brothers via the front door. I opened the bathroom door to see Holly waiting, no Joshes in sight.

"Are you sure you're OK?"

"Yeah, I'm fine." I wasn't sure if it was proper to thank a girl for saving your ass, so I didn't mention it.

"Those guys are real jerks. I can't believe them."

I had no trouble believing it at all. I tried to remain calm, but I couldn't help casting about to see if they were still there, and I suspect Holly noticed. I felt embarrassed.

"Let's go out this way," she suggested and took me by the hand, leading me through a dark hallway to a door that opened to the back side of the bar. The night air was still warm, despite the season, and I felt my shirt clinging to my body. "At least your leg seems better now."

"Huh?" It was hard to hear over the band. We couldn't see them from where we were, but we could hear them banging out their tortured chords.

"Well, I figured that was why you tripped."

I had utterly forgotten my fake injury, but she didn't seem to doubt my sincerity, so I just nodded.

"Maybe when Josh picked you up it popped the knee joint back into place," she laughed, "like some kind of chiropractic manipulation or something." More laughter.

I nodded again. I was becoming profoundly aware of my poor conversational performance with Holly, a performance more embarrassing than my performance in front of the toilet. I was a little shy about talking to her, partially for fear of giving away Milton's double-date scheme, a scheme that required a great deal of attention if it was to be pulled off neatly. While I still doubted that it could be pulled off at all, I felt a certain obligation to uphold my part of the charade. It wouldn't do to have the whole thing blow up because I couldn't manage a little artful, even if slightly deceitful, conversation. But now I remained quiet because of my feeble showing in front of her friends, not at all well done. While I didn't imagine myself as much of a challenge for Josh and his gang, I fancied myself somewhat more capable of maintaining my wits, at least so far as to have offered the cover boy bully a verbal riposte upon being rescued by Holly. Any clever comment would have saved the moment, finishing that nasty business in a neat fashion. "A pleasure to meet you" or "You seem to have a bit of spinach in your teeth" or even "You might want to refresh your deodorant"—though there was some chance that such a remark could result in the beating I had been lucky to avoid. Any comment at all would have done just fine, anything to reassert my existence as resilient to the terrorism of such a thug. But these comments fall within the domain of books and movies, when the danger threatens Cary Grant or Humphrey Bogart. Rarely in reality do we pull them off with style. No, real people just sulk off and mutter to themselves the gem of brilliance that would have proven their worth. At that moment, I felt worthless.

As I contemplated the events that led to my leaning against the hurricane fence behind The Mermaid with Milton's girlfriend Holly, I realized that the toilet incident had been merely the crowning jewel of my first night back in New Orleans. I was tempted to fly home to Boston the next morning.

Holly looked me over. "Why so quiet? You don't seem the strong, silent type to me."

This was followed by less of a laugh than a smirk but didn't seem to demand a response, so I stuck to the no-response-is-a-safe-response routine. She looked away, beyond the abandoned lot behind The Mermaid to the overpass that seemed an accessory to the forsaken neighborhood. I hoped she was done with her interrogation, and I began contemplating what I might say to change the subject. But when you have been silent, it is difficult to start speaking, especially when you want to sound witty.

"You don't seem like Rachael's type either." Apparently she wasn't done. She turned and faced me again. "Where do you two know each other from?"

Had she smoked our charade?

I tried to think, but it was too late for cleverness. I was lost, and the taste of Scotch and bile wasn't helping.

"I don't know, seems like we've known each other forever." A brilliant save, I thought. "We aren't that close, not a serious couple." Ouch, not so well done. I had hoped to deflect any suggestion that we were a perfect match by making it seem as if we were just friends, but the intimation fell flat and came out like a weak attempt to sound available.

Holly looked at me earnestly. I felt like an idiot. She had to know.

"No kidding."

Was she being facetious?

"You hardly said hello to her when she got in the car. I thought it must be a blind date Milton had set you up on or something, since you said you were from Boston."

She hadn't smoked it. In fact, she had completely bought the whole thing and with a very credible explanation. I felt instantly invigorated. Perhaps the whole evening had not been a complete waste.

"No, she's not really my type," I agreed, hoping to convince her of her own account of events.

"What is your type?"

I thought of Jane immediately, and a tide of emotion flooded over me again. The triumph of the double-date charade did little to compensate for that disaster.

"She is already taken," I said.

"Are you sure?" she asked.

"The empirical evidence is overwhelming."

She turned away and looked out across the desolation of the Warehouse District.

"Let's return to the bar," I said. "I will buy you a drink."

"You sound like Milton," she laughed and took my arm. "I'm all yours."

I led her around the side of the building, through the crowd listening to the four girls wailing on stage, and inside The Mermaid's front door.

13

MILTON WAS LEANING OVER THE BAR, pointing to some bottle he presumably wanted to sample. He turned when he saw us approaching and shouted over the band noise that crept in through the cracks under the doors and windows. "Holly, Tim, you drink aquavit, don't you?"

Holly sighed and said to me, "I'll take a rain check on that drink. I am going back to listen to the terrible band." She turned and left.

"What's wrong with her?" Milton asked as I walked up.

"Beats me," I said, "but she hasn't figured out your little ruse yet."

"Totally in the dark, huh?"

"I don't know why it worked, but it did. Somehow, she rationalized the apparent coolness between Rachael and me as the result of our being on a blind date."

"Of course, my lad, this scheme can't fail."

"I am impressed, Milton. I would never have thought such a twisted and unscrupulous plan could succeed. You have really done it."

"Of course it worked. I knew it would work. It could never fail unless someone squealed. The more twisted and unscrupulous, the more likely the success."

"I'm afraid I don't follow you."

"They are my girlfriends. That means they adore me."

He paused and looked at me squarely. "At least they tolerate me," he revised. "The point is simple enough. Who would arrange two dates on the same night and then try to keep them both? The depravity of the thing is so great that it protects me from discovery. Only a confirmed cad could act in such a manner, and by definition, no woman's boyfriend counts as a confirmed cad. For if he did, then he would not be her boyfriend. Like I said, the more unscrupulous, the more likely the success."

"Then this plan is bound to succeed."

"I am pleased that you see the logic in it."

I nodded.

"It is theoretically impossible for them to figure it out on their own. Like asking a person to imagine a color they have never seen."

The drinks he ordered arrived. They were curiously tall and full of ice and a clear liquid.

"What is it?" I asked.

"Aquavit rickey," he pronounced. "An absolutely dreadful drink. Tastes like caraway seed bread. But the Arizona brothers didn't believe that anyone would invent a cocktail that tastes like bad bread, so I had to order a couple to prove it. Would you care for one?"

"No, I am convinced already, but I might have another Scotch," given that the Scotch I had drunk was lost prematurely.

As the bartender fetched it, Milton pointed to the Arizona brothers and said, "They are a great find, true aficionados of my revolutionary plan. These are fellows whom others can look up to."

I wasn't sure what he meant by "look up to," because the white brother had begun to slump in his seat, apparently from drink, and was likely to fall to the ground at any moment. The black brother was still going but seemed less lifelike than before. They appeared to lack Milton's stamina. I figured he would teach them that too.

"How do you plan to get him into the debutante ball?"

"Oh, that's no problem." Milton knew immediately that I meant the pink brother.

"And you think he'll feel comfortable in that environment?"

"What environment?"

"Uh, white, upper-class, snobbish racists."

"Don't you think you are being a little hard on your family's social circle?"

"I'm generalizing, probably unfairly, but didn't it occur to you that he might feel uncomfortable there?"

"My friend, those Arizona brothers are amazing. They can teach you and me a great deal about the world. They have actually transcended their racial identity. By transcended, I don't mean ignored but moved beyond. To describe either of them as white or black would be a terrible discredit to them."

"Oh, don't give me that. You can't walk around this city for more than two hours without being made intimately aware of your race. You don't transcend race. Not in New Orleans, not in this country."

I believe at this point the Bourbon from The Columns was speaking. My thinking lacked the clarity of Scotch, which made sense given that most of it was working its way through the New Orleans sewage system toward the Mississippi River, the source of the city's water supply. I was no authority on race matters. Perhaps race didn't matter. I knew as much about race as the residents of the city knew about the water they drank, but I had always been bothered by it. I never cared about the big issues of race. I was certainly no civil rights activist. If the saying "You are either part of the solution or part of the problem" is true, I was part of the problem. Did that make me a racist? I didn't feel like one. I guess my attitudes on race were simply self-centered. From a strictly selfish standpoint, I didn't like racism because I didn't like people to be unfriendly toward me. And there were a lot of black people who were unfriendly toward me. That is not to say they persecuted me in any way; they just looked at me as if I were the enemy. I didn't want to be anyone's enemy. If treating people fairly meant that they would be nice to me, I was willing to do it. But it didn't seem to matter how I treated people. I felt as though my relationship with black people was defined by someone else, something else, culture perhaps. But whose culture? Certainly not a culture that I created. So how did it stick to us all so effectively? Perhaps some great-great-second uncle of mine was a slave owner, and perhaps he had beaten his slaves. And perhaps, as a result of lineage, I should be identified as the oppressor. Well, if that were so, I wish the son of a bitch hadn't beaten them so hard. I was paying for my hypothetical great-great-uncle's sins, all society was paying for them, and it looked like we would continue to pay for a long time. Everyone was still talking about racism, and everyone was still pointing fingers, and somehow I was in the middle of it. Now the bourbon was not only talking for me but thinking for me too. I decided not to share my confused views on race with Milton.

"That, my friend, is because you don't understand transcendence," Milton continued. "They have surpassed the limits of racial identity."

"Yeah, well some limits aren't self-imposed. Jim Crow laws weren't self-imposed."

"My dear friend, the days of Jim Crow are over. Somehow we have all been convinced of this German notion of a social consciousness—the idea that a society has a spirit that maintains attitudes and prejudices and that these attitudes persist despite changes in individuals or the law. Well, it is nonsense. The argument defeats itself. If these prejudices are human, they must be expressed by individual humans, not society. There is no such thing as a social mind. I defy any sociologist out there to find a social mind. There are only social individuals, and individual prejudices can be transcended by the individuals expressing them. Of course, that doesn't mean that the attitudes of others disappear, but we can't be responsible for everyone else anyway, can we?"

"That works until someone attacks you, beats you up, hangs you from a tree."

"If that is your standard for racism, then I am certain your parents are innocent. Your parents are good citizens, pay their taxes, and raised their children to vote Republican. What more would you have them do?"

Was it true? I wondered. Surely William voted Republican, but Sarah, Tabatha?

Milton continued. "But I suspect it is not truly the violence that concerns you."

"How so?" I asked.

"Violence and prejudice are two completely different things."

"I don't follow you." I was confused.

"Does somebody have to be racially motivated to beat you up?"

I reflected upon Josh and his bathroom buddies. "No."

"Then violence and prejudice are not identical. They are separate things. They may occasionally come together, like sunshine and rain, but nobody is stupid enough to think the sun causes the rain."

"Sunshine and rain?"

"You know, the Devil beating his wife?"

"Of course."

"You have seen it rain when the sun was out?"

"Every summer. I thought it was a New Orleans phenomenon."

Milton shook his head. "You need to travel more. Anyway, the old lady who lives next door to me always says, 'The Devil is beating his wife,' when it happens.

Now, we would never accuse the Devil of being a racist for beating his wife, would we?"

I knew Milton was confusing this metaphor on purpose, so that I would have to point out the confused metaphor to finish the argument. But only a witless drone would have failed to see what he was doing. To win the argument, you had to show yourself to be a witless drone—or a know-it-all Yankee condemning the entire South for its racism and ignorance. Such condemnations were common but unlikely to fly against two brothers from Arizona. But I wasn't prepared to allow Milton to win the argument so easily. I pressed through the bourbon, Paisano, and Scotch to make a singular and deadly strike against his position.

"How does this existentialist attitude toward individual transcendence vogue with your Marxist worldview?"

"Oh, that? Don't mind that. I assure you it vogues perfectly well. It just works in reverse. The revolution requires individuals to recognize the evils of capital and then convince other individuals to recognize it too. There is no mindless social upheaval. The revolution must be carried out by individuals, who else?"

I was not convinced, but his argument worked and I couldn't put together five more words in a row that would make sense. I tested the Scotch—still very good— and suggested we join the brothers. Milton ignored me and continued rambling about their transcendence.

"To be black without being black. Does that mean acting white? No. That wouldn't be transcendence. That would just be role-playing. But being black is role-playing too. Being black is identical with being white.

Who told black people they were black? White people. No, a black man can't embrace blackness without playing a role dictated to him by white men."

"Where do you get this stuff?" I asked.

"I, too, was ignorant until I met the brothers. They have taught me much. Much that is crucial for the revolution, because the revolution will require both black and white participants. You know, there are a lot more poor people in this country than rich people, but the rich keep the poor divided over racial issues."

I had heard this before and told Milton, but he kept going.

"These racial issues prevent anyone from seeing the real problem. James Baldwin knew it. Martin Luther King knew it. Remember the Poor People's Campaign? What was that if not the Marxist revolution come to the shores of America? And it wasn't but a couple weeks later that King got shot. The wealthy knew that as long as King focused on civil rights for the Negroes, racism would persist and distract Americans from the real problem. But once that Poor People's Campaign began, something had to be done, and they shot him."

"They?" I asked, thinking I had caught him. "Is that not a social mind?"

"Of course not. Someone pulled the trigger, but it doesn't matter who did it or why. The anti-revolutionary forces won."

"What's this got to do with the brothers?" I asked but immediately regretted doing so. I wasn't sure whom Milton meant by "they." Did he mean white people? Did he mean rich people? In fact, I didn't care whom he meant. I was convinced that he was too drunk to drive this conversation. While I contemplated this, Milton jettisoned that "they" and introduced another.

"Because they have actually moved past that tired, old capitalist dichotomy. Once you realize that the danger lies in celebrating diversity, you can save yourself. Diversity is nonsense. There is no diversity. There are only rich people and poor people. What do all the poor black folks in the ghetto complain about? They complain that when someone succeeds and leaves the ghetto, these nouveaux riches forget about their friends still in the ghetto. They forget because they are rich. Rich and poor, the real dichotomy."

I wasn't sure why he was telling me this, and his aquavit rickeys were beginning to sweat.

"You don't know why I am telling you this, do you?" Milton asked.

"No."

"Because you are in the same situation. You see everything as white or black, wrong or right. You think people who make decisions that differ from your own are wrong."

"No, I don't."

"Perhaps not wrong, but not as good. You're an incurable snob."

"No more so than you," I quipped. "What about your revolution? You obviously think you are right and everyone else is wrong."

"Yeah, but at least I believe it."

I was confused and didn't want to be enlightened, but my habit of curiosity still exceeded my intoxication, and so the question slipped out. "What are you talking about?"

"I know I am a snob, but I like being a snob. I have worked very hard at it. I also believe that I am right and that everyone else is wrong. But you—I don't understand you, Tim. You're a snob, but you hate snobbery. You can't commit to anything. Make a decision! Take a stand! Don't worry about whether it is right or wrong."

Milton paused from his ranting for a moment, looked me in the eye, and said, "My honest opinion and my friendly advice is this: Do it or do not do it—you will regret it either way."

He was right, of course. I always regretted my decisions, whether made thoughtfully or thoughtlessly. There didn't seem to be a mechanism for avoiding regret. Was this true of me, or was it true of everyone?

"What about the girls?" I decided to change the subject.

"What girls?"

"Our, I mean, your dates."

"Oh, I am sure they are fine. They're big girls. I am far more concerned about the Arizona brothers. You know, they can't really handle their liquor, as evidenced by the K-car."

The brothers looked like a train wreck. The white brother had finally sunk to the floor, leaving the other stretched between the abandoned chair and his own.

"These drinks will perk them up." We got up and carried the clear, cold, caraway cocktails to the dazed brothers. Milton helped the supine one, while I assisted the other in sitting up and wrapping his hands around the glass.

"Drink this," I said.

He looked at me like a Judas, so I added, "Milton assures me that it will revive you."

Now I felt like a Judas, but upon mentioning Milton's name he smiled and pressed his lips against the glass. Milton had lifted the other brother, who was now gulping down the caraway concoction.

The chill of the liquor seemed to have an initial soothing effect, but the caraway aftertaste must have kicked in shortly thereafter. The black brother had a violent reaction, spitting most of his drink across the table.

"Sweet Jesus, what the hell is that crap?" he shouted and continued to spit. Milton just laughed.

"It's the happy flavor of caraway seeds," Milton trumpeted.

The black brother turned to his white brother to see if he had fared better. The white brother was drinking it down like soda.

"Dude, are you numb?" the black brother asked.

"No, I like caraway seeds."

"Caraway seeds? You like that crap? What kind of Jewish, caraway-eating freak are you?"

I turned quickly to Milton and whispered, "Jewish?"

Milton shook his head subtly, keeping his eyes on the brothers.

"So much for his transcending racial barriers," I said.

"Hush and watch," he said to me. To the brothers, he said, "The aquavit rickey is not Jewish. It's a Scandinavian drink."

"Scanda-freakin-navian? Jewish? What's the difference? Anyone who drinks this kinda crap must be from some freaking weirdo place."

"But I am from Arizona," defended the aquavit-drinking brother.

"Can you prove it?" asked the other and eyed him close. I became bored and returned to the bar for a drink. Milton stayed to watch.

I ordered another Scotch. Roberto joined me.

"Are the Arizona brothers drunk yet?" he asked me.

"Yes." It was the first straight answer I had given in a long time.

"They will start fighting soon."

"Fighting, no, they are too drunk to fight."

"No, the brothers, they will fight. They always fight. They are from Arizona."

"People from Arizona fight?"

"Well, I don't really know. They are the only people from Arizona I have ever met. But they certainly fight a lot."

My drink came, and I attended to it immediately. Roberto shook his head in disapproval. "You shouldn't drown your sorrows in that stuff. There are so many beautiful women here. Why can you not find comfort with one of them? Is this other woman so different from these?"

I looked about the crowded bar—a freak show if there ever was one.

"Yes," I said happily and sincerely. I was beginning to like Roberto. He was an easy man to talk to, even if his English was somewhat stilted. I heard a crash and saw the brothers rolling on the floor. First the chairs, then the table went over. Milton made no effort to separate them. He didn't even get up.

"There they go," Roberto added as he ordered a glass of wine. The bouncer arrived, and the brothers were soon out the door. "Good-bye, my friend. I hope you solve your problem."

Milton waltzed over and told me to drink up. "We are going to the Quarter."

When I got to the car, the girls were already squeezed into the backseat with the now much calmer brothers. Milton started the car and announced, "To The Royal Orleans!"

THE ROYAL ORLEANS

The only time I ever said no to a drink
was when I misunderstood the question.

Will Sinclair

MARTINI

2 OZ DRY GIN
¼ OZ DRY VERMOUTH

Combine ingredients in a
cocktail shaker with ice.
Strain into a martini glass.
Add an olive or lemon peel.

14

APPARENTLY, "TO THE ROYAL ORLEANS" didn't actually mean that we were going to The Royal Orleans, at least not directly. With the music blasting, the six of us rocketed down Camp Street into the heart of the city: the French Quarter. I was dreading it. I had never cared much for the French Quarter myself, a hot, stinky place full of tourists, expensive bars, shabby strip clubs, and shops that sold adult novelty T-shirts. I especially never understood the T-shirt industry. Who wears a shirt that says, "Shuck me, suck me, eat me raw"? What occasion is appropriate? As I saw it, there was nothing I could get downtown that I couldn't get uptown, except perhaps AIDS or robbed or murdered or all three.

"Why are we going downtown?" I asked in a very loud, very whiny voice.

Milton turned from the heads-up display windshield. "Downtown is where it's at," he shouted over the music.

"Why don't you drop me off at Canal Street? I'll take the streetcar home."

Milton gave me an evil look, leaned across the seat, and delivered his comment directly into my ear. "You can't go home without your date, and which one would that be?"

This seemed to be his problem, not mine, but I was too drunk to find my way home alone. I imagined that I could survive a visit to the French Quarter and resigned myself to it, nodding my halfhearted approval.

"You won't regret it, I promise."

I already did.

As it was Friday night, parking would be impossible, the exception being parking on Rampart Street, where your car was certain to be stolen and you mugged as you departed or returned. Milton drove directly to Rampart, parked the car, instructed us to leave the doors unlocked, and hurried us into the bowels of the Quarter. Nobody seemed nervous except me.

Milton put his hand on my arm. "Relax, Tim, nobody will steal that car," he pointed back at the K-car, which looked like the loser of a demolition derby, "and we have no money, so we are safe as well."

"I have money," I said in a worried tone.

"Oh yeah. I forgot."

I growled.

"We will make sure you don't have any left by the time we return."

We turned off Rampart onto Conti Street. Milton announced to our little gang, "I hope you all brought your bathing suits, but first, The Bombay Club."

Holly wandered over to Rachel. "Have you been to The Bombay Club?"

"No," answered Rachel. She was prepared to say more, but Milton interrupted her.

"The Bombay Club is inside the Prince Conti Hotel," he explained as if the girls were interested.

Holly ignored Milton and asked Rachel, "Did you attend Ursuline Academy?"

"Yes."

"Then you might know my friend Alison Bechdel—" but Milton intervened again.

"We must cross Burgundy and Dauphine and then look for the flags," he instructed. The girls abandoned their effort at conversation.

The Prince Conti Hotel appeared suddenly before us, exactly where Milton had predicted it would be, and there, safely nestled inside of it, lay The Bombay Club. The barroom was air-conditioned, and although the December night was warm and muggy, inside you could see your breath. I was glad to have the suit jacket. I considered surrendering it to one of the girls, but my chivalry was happily cut short by this double-date dilemma. To whom do I give the jacket? I was beginning to appreciate the dynamics of this date more and more. Apart from the temperature, the place was glorious: darkly stained wood surrounded by heavy leather chairs and couches. Against the left wall were handsome booths with deep red draperies for privacy. Rachel pointed at one of the booths and whispered something to Holly, which made Holly laugh. The place was almost empty, only two men in suits at the bar drinking martinis and smoking large cigars. The Arizona brothers sat together on a leather couch facing a sizable coffee table. There were two leather chairs on the opposite side. Milton offered the chairs to the girls, pulled another one up for me, and then sat on the couch next to the blue brother. Had he orchestrated that in advance with the brothers?

The waiter arrived, and Milton ordered martinis for everyone. "My treat," he said and asked each of us if we preferred them straight up or on the rocks. Only the brothers took them on the rocks. "Rocks, dude," one said. I presumed that it was an Arizona thing.

The first martini went down hard. Perhaps it was my body trying to warn me that the gin would not make pleasant bedfellows with its already imbibed kissing cousins. I was not the only one having trouble with it, because there wasn't much talk until the second round came. Then the conversation and the martinis began to flow. Milton was busy discussing his dissertation topic with Rachel, something about modern poor people's movements and the lack of theoretical support being their downfall.

"You must have the intellectuals on board in any revolution. The poor are the body of the revolution, the intellectuals are the mind. Most movements lack one of these parts and, hence, cannot sustain themselves. I am working on the theoretical model for modern revolutions, but one must not merely think. The thinker must act as well. So in addition to my philosophical work, I am also laying the groundwork for the body of the revolution."

I knew that his body of the revolution was sitting in the room, right there in front of him. This was it, two drunken Arizona brothers, two teenage girls, and one friend from out of town. I wanted to point that out to him, but I didn't. Having heard his views on overthrowing capitalism through consumer debt, I also wanted to add that the mental component of his revolution was as flimsy as its body. I remained silent on that as well. Still, Rachel was an attentive listener, seemingly impressed by it all. Perhaps it was just a good upbringing. She kept nodding and twirling her fine, gold necklace with her fine, porcelain fingers. They were a girl's fingers: carefree, unadorned with paint or rings. I wanted to touch them. I looked again at Milton. He was still talking about his dissertation, oblivious of the fingers. Did he know those fingers? How did he feel about them? Did he love them? Did he love Holly too? Obviously he didn't love them, not both of them. I tried to imagine being in love with two women at once. I suppose in some way I had always loved Jane, and yet, while I was in Boston, I had fallen in love with Margaret. Did that mean I stopped loving Jane?

More martinis arrived, and the pink brother made a toast to Key West. We all drank.

Perhaps my love for Margaret temporarily eclipsed my love for Jane. Now that Margaret was gone, had my love for Jane returned? Perhaps it wasn't love. Surely it wasn't love.

I looked at Holly, listening to the Arizona brothers talk about Key West. They were describing a girl they knew there. From what I could gather, one of the brothers had stayed with this girl in her parents' house for three months, spending his days by the pool trying to find himself. I wasn't following the conversation very well. Like Rachel, Holly was a good listener. She was absorbed with the story and asked pointed questions to which she got enthusiastic answers. I couldn't keep her questions straight, so the answers were meaningless to me. I looked for her hands, too, her fingers. They were in her hair, long and thin, a perfect symbol of youth. I looked at Milton and marveled. Was it possible? Did he love them both? Of course loving more than one person is possible. I loved my mother, my sisters, my father, all at once. I suppose in some sick way I even loved my brother. If I could love all those people at once, why not two women? What was the difference? The answer, naturally, was sex. For some reason, adding sex to love was supposed to make the love unique. You could only have sexual love with one person at a time. Sexy love with more than one person becomes lust, which is sex without the love. If it was the sex that required devotion to one person and not the love, since you can love parents, sisters, aunts, and uncles, ad infinitum, then why was it the sexuality that remained rather than the love when you were in love with two women? Why did we feel the need to devalue sexual love for two different people and call it lust? It didn't make any sense to me. If you could experience the regular love for more than one person at a time, then why not the sexy love? I wasn't sure why it mattered to me at this moment. Unlike Milton, I did not have the too-many-women problem. I had no women. Milton didn't seem worried about it at all. He was still talking about the revolution. Could the philosophy department at Tulane accept such a thesis? I would have to remember to ask Milton what his advisers thought of the whole thing, but that question would keep.

At some point, the waiter brought the check and a final round. I offered to pay, but Milton pointed at the bill. There was no total. The waiter had written in red marker, "*Viva la revolucion*." Milton stood up, raised his glass in the air, and addressed the entire bar.

"To the revolution and to my friends!"

Milton's revolutionary gang, and several of the bar staff, cheered.

"Stefan's party will be starting soon, and we are expected." Milton tilted his glass and drained the remainder. "Follow me!"

I had no idea who Stefan was.

15

STEFAN'S PARTY HAD ALREADY BEGUN. Milton explained to me that Stefan was from Potsdam, a small East German town just outside of Berlin. With the collapse of the wall, Stefan had come to Tulane to pursue graduate work in physics. It turned out that for Stefan studying physics held fewer challenges than pursuing American girls. So he took a large, second-floor apartment in the French Quarter to use as a command center for his romantic activities. The apartment was on the quiet end of the Quarter, but Stefan was working to fix that. Billie Holiday emanated from the tall, thin windows, and the tall, long-haired, black-leather-wearing guests had poured out into the streets. Only Milton could see over these giants. We pushed through the crowded entranceway to the building, up the crowded stairs, and into the very crowded apartment.

If the guests were bohemians, the apartment was spartan. There was no furniture in the splendid living room that had sixteen-foot ceilings, hardwood floors, and four tremendous windows that stretched from ceiling to floor. A large, Coleman camping lantern hanging precariously from a nail in the wall provided a dull orange glow that mingled with the dappled yellow streetlight to produce a sickly saffron ambiance. The European bohemians were swaying back and forth as if in a group trance. I thought they must all be drunk. It was a little scary. I felt a delicate hand grip the back of my shirt. Was it Rachel, Holly, a bohemian? I couldn't tell in the crowd.

"Are they all drunk?" I asked Milton, who was leading us through the throng.

"They are dancing," he answered.

"To Billie Holiday?"

"They are doing the best they can. The German spirit lusts for soul, but alas," he gestured to the dancers. "Sad, isn't it?" He smiled broadly. "We will fix it."

"Milton!" a distinctly German voice pierced the music. Stefan looked like a praying mantis with a ponytail. He pushed a number of bohemians aside and leaped into the midst of our revolutionary gang. "Thank God you are here. I thought you had forgotten. Did you bring the tape?"

Milton told him he did, but Stefan remained tense. The German introduced himself and apologized for the absence of beer—and his roommate, who had been sent out to buy beer and had disappeared. Stefan shrugged nervously, so as to suggest that both beer and roommates were quite naturally beyond his control, and then invited us to dance, but none of us was eager to join a bunch of sweaty foreigners barely moving to Billie Holiday. There was no beer, the apartment was hot and crowded, and the volume of the music made conversation impossible. I suggested to Milton that we leave.

Milton shook his head no. "Providence put us here for a reason," he shouted so that the brothers and the girls could hear him also. "We must work together."

He looked at the Arizona brothers. "Take the girls. Get beer, as much as you can! Tim will fix the lighting. I will fix the music."

Each brother grabbed a girl by the arm and led them out the way we came. The mystery hand clinging to my shirt was gone.

"What is wrong with the lighting?"

Milton shouted in my ear. "It is boring and a fire hazard. There should be a spiraling disco light mounted on top of a defunct halogen lamppost in Andrew's room—Stefan's roommate. No telling where he is, but that is not our problem. He's a freak anyway. Some English chap who came to Tulane for a grad program in English literature. It makes no sense to me. Anyway, find the disco light and kill that lantern before some long-armed German girl knocks it over and burns the whole block down."

Without further explanation, Milton turned and wandered off into the crowd. I stood there for a moment and then decided that I might as well complete my task.

I pressed through the multitude of hands, butts, and bellies, of breasts, chests, and backsides, a swaying sea of behemoth bohemians. By following the ceiling, I was able to discover a hallway leading past a small kitchen to three doors. The long line outside one told me it was the bathroom. I would have to guess which of the other two rooms was Andrew's. I chose the first. I was wrong.

Stefan was sitting on his bed, with a barefoot bohemian girl, smoking marijuana. The bed was surrounded by heaps of furniture, presumably the furniture that typically occupied the rest of the apartment. I tried to leave gracefully, but Stefan insisted that I join them. He remained outwardly troubled, rubbing his hands together in a circle and repeatedly wiping his brow with the back of one hand. He nervously explained that he needed a few minutes of refuge in his room, away from the crowd, and recommended that I do the same.

"Thank God Milton is finally here," he said, reassuring himself and presumably me. I was not reassured but hated to refuse anyone's hospitality. I stepped over a coffee table, pushed a standing lamp aside, and sat down on an old red couch pressed against the bed. Stefan was explaining to the girl his decision to quit physics. He said it had become meaningless for him. I wasn't particularly interested in his definition of meaninglessness, and trapped as I was by the lamp and coffee table, I decided to take the offensive.

"What did you study?"

"I was working on gravity waves." He produced another joint from his bedside table, lit it, drew heavily, and then offered it to me. I declined.

"Gravity waves?" asked the shoeless girl. I had never heard of them either.

"Yeah, gravity waves. Nobody has proven that they exist. I was part of a study trying to demonstrate their existence."

"How do you prove the existence of gravity waves?" I asked.

"It isn't very easy. Actually, I don't know how you do it, since we never succeeded, but I can tell you what we did."

The shoeless girl reached the end of her joint, leaned back against a pillow, and said, "Gravity waves."

Stefan turned to me. "We got this huge cylinder of nickel, about the size of a compact car. Then we got it really cold, near absolute zero."

"Absolute zero?" I didn't think you could get to absolute zero, or at least that is what I learned in high school.

"Well, close to absolute zero," Stefan clarified. "Anyway, it takes almost a month to get the thing cold enough, then you unpack it and hook it up to the instruments and wait for a supernova to go off somewhere in the universe. If a supernova goes off, then it should emit a bunch of gravity waves, and those waves would be detectable as they strike the metal cylinder."

"Wow." I was really impressed. "How often do supernovas go, well, supernova?"

"Not very often, and since there is no predicting these things, you just get the cylinder cold and hope you get lucky, because it will only stay cold for about a week."

He smoked more, braced himself against the headboard, and looked at the ceiling. The shoeless girl put her head on his lap.

"There were a bunch of these cylinders around the world at different universities, each doing more or less the same thing, trying to detect gravity waves. We worked on this dumb thing for months without a single supernova. Then one day, while we had the cylinder all packed up trying to get it cold, we hear about a super nova going off."

He smoked some more and passed the remainder to the girl.

"Of course, we were helpless to do anything because our cylinder wasn't cold enough yet. So my professor gets on the phone to his colleagues in Australia to see if their cylinder was ready. They were icing their cylinder too. So he calls all the other detection sites. They were all warm."

Stefan repeated himself as if he thought we didn't get it. "Not a single, cold cylinder of nickel on the planet. All these stupid cylinder sites all over the world, and they are all down at once. When we finally get a supernova, nobody is ready."

"Seems like they would coordinate their efforts," added the girl.

"They do now, but I was done with it. I had completely lost my faith in the whole scientific establishment. So I quit."

"He's an idealist," the girl said, looking at him dreamily.

"Well, I quit working. I am still enrolled, I still have a student visa, and I still get a graduate stipend, but I no longer consider myself a scientist."

"Why?"

"We thought that the discovery of gravity waves would help illustrate Einstein's theory of relativity and possibly lead to a theory of everything. But we were *auf dem Holzweg*, as we say in Germany."

"Barking up the wrong tree?" I asked.

"Exactly," he said, now feeling encouraged. "This sort of meta-questioning can only be put in such a way that the questioner, as such, is, by his very questioning, involved in the question."

"You mean," I started tentatively, trying to work out his logic, "that when we ask a question about the nature of the universe, we are really asking a question about our nature?" I paused, and then it came to me. "Because a question of that sort expresses a particular relationship to the universe," and I finished with a flourish, "and it is that relationship that we are truly questioning."

Stefan raised an eyebrow at me. "I meant that you cannot distill the order of the universe from the disorder of man."

This story was beginning to sound familiar. No wonder Stefan was friendly with Milton. They were both living comfortably on the graduate student welfare system.

Stefan had illustrated to me what I feared the most: a world in chaos. In the rest of the United States, everything seemed to work. At least, everyone thinks things work. This is especially true in Boston, where hard work appears to generate results and everyone believes in science and culture. But in New Orleans, the dark underbelly of the country, nothing functions the way it should. Science and culture fail, and nobody expects them to succeed. Nobody has faith in science or hard work. The question was: Which perspective is correct? Had the rest of the country been hoodwinked, fooled into false optimism, or were the people in New Orleans merely incompetent and morbidly pessimistic? I obviously didn't know, but I was starting to side with the pessimists. I wondered where the German Stefan stood.

"What are you now?" I couldn't help my curiosity. How did Stefan define his current state? He shared Milton's indolent idealism. Was he a revolutionary too?

"I am just hanging out in the French Quarter, drinking beer, and smoking a little dope."

How pathetic, I thought, but the thought was accompanied by a hint of doubt.

"How cool," said the girl, passing the joint back to him.

"I have got to get a disco lamp. Thank you for your hospitality."

Stefan turned to me, showing a flash of nervousness. "Is Milton taking care of the music?"

"He said so." I stood up from the couch, snaked my way past the various pieces of furniture, and exited the room, leaving a cloud of smoke behind me.

I went to the remaining door. What I saw there was no more settling than what I had just left. In addition to a dining room table and chairs that I assumed were not normally located here, Andrew's room looked like it had been used as a snow globe. There were two disheveled dressers, each with the drawers either open or out on the floor, and clothing strewn about the room. The bed was covered with books, magazines, and a motor scooter that was missing the front wheel. At each corner of the bed stood waist-high candlesticks, complete with half-burnt white candles. From beneath the bed protruded the naked legs of a mannequin, with some sort of scribbling on them. Closer inspection showed that the scribbling was poetry—more accurately, one poem, written over and over again on the legs. The poem was Robert Herrick's "Upon Julia's Clothes." Each edition was inscribed in a different fashion, different style or shape. The temptation to pull the legs out from under the bed to discover the remainder of the mannequin was great. I resisted. Directly above me hung a Union Jack. The flag had about twenty signatures on it. I figured they were probably members of a national soccer team. Under the window sat five clay pots with light-starved marijuana plants. On one wall was a closed closet door. Against the other wall, there was a mirror that had been painted with flowers. And next to the mirror was a spiraling disco lamp mounted on a long black pole. I stepped toward the light and heard a moan come from the closet. I stopped and looked for an object with which to defend myself in the event that the moan belonged to something dangerous. I chose a candlestick. It was sticky. I set it back down and wiped my hands on the sheets of the bed. A second moan was followed by a third that sounded more like "Om." Was the thing meditating? I decided not to stick around to see. I leaped through the clutter, grabbed the lamp, and started for the door. The closet door opened, and there, pressed in with the clothing, was a naked man. He gave me an awkward look and then closed the door. I left with the lamp.

In the hall, I ran into Stefan leading the barefoot bohemian girl out of his room. I grabbed him by the arm. "There's a naked man in Andrew's closet."

"Probably Andrew," but Stefan was not giving me his full attention. He looked even more nervous now, rubbing his hands together and casting about, as if fearful of an unseen predator. He kept standing on the tips of his toes, looking into the living room over the crowd of people.

"What is going on in there?" he asked, but not to anyone in particular, certainly not me.

"Is he dangerous?" I asked.

Stefan nodded and then turned to me with alarm, as if he had just noticed my presence.

"The music?"

Billie Holiday had gone silent and been replaced by bohemian conversation. "Milton said he was going to take care of the music. What is he doing?" Stefan was now in full panic.

The poor bastard couldn't endure the social pressures of his own party. Perhaps he was afraid his guests would not enjoy themselves and his inability to amuse them would reveal that he was only pretending to be bohemian or whatever it was he thought he was. He had left the weighty world of science to pursue the light world of beer drinking and dope smoking. Perhaps he feared a dull party would reveal that beneath his new French Quarter veneer was but classic German angst. Angst that had its roots in the science of Kant, Hegel, Freud, Heisenberg, and Einstein, the scientific music of Beethoven, the scientific anti-science of Nietzsche, and the scientific totalitarianism of Hitler. It's what made the Germans deep thinkers, but it also made them anxious. The collective German spirit was racked with this anxiety—though Milton was sure to take umbrage with my depiction of such social consciousness. Maybe Stefan had tried to escape this scientific dread, but he would have to convince others of a successful escape in order to convince himself. No doubt a party of German conversation runs the risk of becoming very serious and very melancholy, and it was easy to see that this and every party he threw for the rest of his life could conjure these self-doubts. I began to feel sorry for him, without even knowing for sure what it was I was sorry about.

I felt sorry for Andrew too. Poor Andrew had probably been infected with Stefan's seriousness and angst. The English psyche was, after all, only a short walk from the German spirit. Then again, maybe Stefan and Andrew were displaying a perfectly normal reaction to this gathering, a soirée that seemed more likely to be the product of Milton's handiwork than either the nervous German or naked Englishman. Perhaps it was just the gin and whiskey that made this entire event seem unreal and insignificant to me.

With the spiral disco lamp in my hand, I pressed past Stefan and his barefoot girl into the congested living room. The conversation that had replaced the music was about the lack of music. Everyone was miffed and expressing displeasure. I heard one tall Aryan fellow say, "Stefan said the music was going to rock. This is lame." I hoped Stefan couldn't hear them. I couldn't see where I was going, but I kept moving in the direction of the lantern light.

"Goddamn, Timothy!" It was Milton, of course. "Do something before Christmas!"

I couldn't see Milton, but I knew he could see me and was wondering where the hell I had been. On a voyage through the depths of the tortured German soul, I wanted to tell him, but instead I continued an impossible beeline for the lantern. I reached the wall, pushed a tall girl in a leather skirt out of the way, found a socket, and plugged in the disco light. The flickering orange beam of the lantern was replaced by swirling purple paisleys and psychedelic flowers: from Plato's cave to Travolta's paradise. A hush ran over the crowd. I felt a shudder of anticipation. Then I heard Milton's voice again, but this time it was amplified by the stereo system speakers. He spoke softly into a microphone, and, through the miracle of modern audio technology, his deep, reverberating voice carried throughout the now quiet apartment and into the street as if he were a famous baritone at La Scala.

"Ladies and gentlemen, *meine Damen und Herren*, welcome to the revolution. Your credit cards have no limit here."

There were loud cheers. Milton waited until the cheers stopped. He waited some more, holding the microphone close to his lips as if prepared to speak, but saying nothing. He allowed the anticipation to build. What was he waiting to say? I felt myself holding my breath. An instant before the partygoers despaired of an answer or I passed out, Soft Cell's "Tainted Love" burst upon us like a summer rain. These bohemians knew exactly what to do. As if choreographed, the whole group fell into frenzied dancing on the fifth beat. The temperature in the apartment soared, and the dancers began flinging off their hip bohemian jackets and scarves, their hats and their gloves, their vests and their belts, their boots and their socks. Before the final chorus, they looked less like hip bohemians than a bunch of first-time students in an aerobics class. The dancing spread down the stairs into the street, like an earthquake pulsing outward from its epicenter. That epicenter was Milton, whirling and jumping in the middle of the room. "Tainted Love" blended into "My Sharona." A genre shift for sure, but the crowd never missed a beat.

I stepped away from the wall and was immediately drawn into the fray. I jumped and spun and threw my arms about with wild abandon, with no care for whom I might collide with. We were not slam-dancing. There was no violence or aggression, but neither was I fearful of physical contact with the other dancers. We pressed together, like a single body, half-naked, whirling and spinning and jumping. By the end of "My Sharona," I had worked up a pretty good sweat. Maybe it was slam-dancing. In the midst of it all, I had hung my jacket on the nail that held the lantern and stuffed my tie into my pants pocket. I had no idea where my shoes and socks were. I heard cheering and turned to see the naked Andrew, now painted bright red from head to toe, dancing on top of what must have been a table or box that he dragged from his room for this particular purpose. The dancers moved around Andrew in a circle, making great primordial sounds. I could see Stefan, the praying mantis of a man, now dancing and thumping and shouting with the rest of them, his seriousness and anxiety forgotten for the moment. I collided with Milton, who immediately produced a primal bellow of his own. I shouted back a caveman-like call that left a huge grin on my face.

This was New Orleans. This was graduate school as I had recalled it. Not a perpetual dance party but freedom, the freedom of limbo. When you're no longer really a student, even though you attend the university, and you are not working, even though you're not unemployed. You are nothing—but a situated nothing that enjoys insulation from the demands of modern life by a thousand-year-old pursuit of wisdom. You are free; you are freedom. The internal limitations, naturally, still exist, and for me, those were plentiful and powerful. But the rigor-less, unstructured schedule of the graduate student, along with the free flow of alcohol in a city where the bars never close, offered infinite opportunities for one to shed those mind-forged manacles. Helen had been another expression of my freedom, but the shame of that event had caused me to flee grad school. In leaving, I had unintentionally left behind those opportunities for freedom, opportunities that so rarely presented themselves in the northern nine-to-five world I now occupied. Worse still, in three years, I hadn't noticed the loss. Boston, the new job, freezing temperatures, and a fiancée who didn't pronounce Rs had distracted me, kept me busy. I had lost myself and didn't notice. But here, in the French Quarter, surrounded by half-naked bohemians and too drunk to spell my own name, I had found myself again. I hoped that in the morning I would remember the self that had returned.

Somebody handed me a beer, which could only mean that the Arizona brothers and my dates were back. The beer was cold and sharp. I absorbed it like a dry sponge and immediately wanted another. Fresh air blew in from the open windows, tall enough to allow a man in half a gray suit to stand up straight in the opening. I stepped onto the broad windowsill. Billy Idol's "Dancing with Myself" engulfed me. The bohemians dancing in the street saw me and shouted encouragement, so I resumed moving to the music, now by myself in the window. I saw the white Arizona brother straddling a plastic bucket filled with beer and ice at the edge of the dancers. He was passing out beer as fast as he could. I needed one of those beers. I felt the thirst boiling up from deep within me. I shouted to him, but the music was much too loud.

I saw Holly dancing in the street, directly below me. She looked up and waved. I shouted to her to come up, but she couldn't hear me either. She motioned for me to come down. I jumped.

BRUNCH

The office of the leisure class in social evolution is to
retard movement and conserve what is obsolescent.

Thorstein Veblen

MILK PUNCH

2 OZ BRANDY
½ C WHOLE MILK
½ C CREAM
1 OZ SIMPLE SYRUP
1 DASH VANILLA EXTRACT

Shake ingredients together with ice in a cocktail shaker for one minute. Strain into a rocks glass with crushed ice. Dust with nutmeg.

16

THE BALE OF COTTON IN MY MOUTH did little to distract from the throbbing in my head that woke me. It was morning, but only just, and I felt as if I had slept for only ten minutes. I searched for my watch but it wasn't there—wrong arm. I attempted the other arm but found it under something, someone, some woman, some girl.

"Oh God," slipped out before I could silence myself. She remained asleep. I lay back and stared at the ceiling. I couldn't tell at first whether it was the bed or the ceiling fan that was spinning. It was the bed. Think, damn it, think. There was nothing, except a little anxiety over my whereabouts and the mystery girl beside me. I tried harder.

I looked again at the pile of hair next to me. Blonde, pretty, but who was she and where was I? I concentrated again on the ceiling fan, trying to block out the haze left over from what? I wasn't sure of the source. Was it bourbon? The thought of bourbon triggered my gag reflex—must have been bourbon. Years ago, I had discovered that I could determine the cause of a hangover by imagining all the likely suspects. When I hit the correct one, my body convulsed. But I also had something of a beer aftertaste in my mouth. Wow, more gagging with the thought of beer. Wine? Ugh, gag. Only through great concentration was I able to keep the contents of my stomach where they belonged. I was beginning to grow nervous. What the hell had I been doing all night? I tried again. Tequila? Nothing. Thank God, tequila hangovers would invariably leave me on the toilet all day. Scotch? Oh yes, a bit of a twinge there too. Gin?

"Ack," I said and swallowed whatever it was that had leaped from my intestines into the back of my throat. I decided that I couldn't go further with my experiment without risk to the bed and the girl. It was a lovely, feminine bed, with white, frilly sheets. But how had I gotten in it?

Yesterday morning, I had woken in my own bed, in my own apartment in Boston, lying next to nobody but myself. I remembered eggs and bacon for breakfast—you can't count on the breakfast promised by the airline— and throwing my suitcases into the back of what must have been the only cab in Boston that wasn't heated. It was the crack of dawn in December, and the cab felt like a meat locker. I got on an airplane, ate that breakfast too, since it also was eggs and bacon, and twenty-four hours later here I was in a strange bed, in a strange house, and no notion of how any of it had come to be. And the girl—who was she? My mind wandered over the ceiling fan and my second breakfast on the plane, but no further details of the evening revealed themselves to me. Had I really drunk that much? Another gag reflex. I had to do something, but not knowing where I was, it wasn't clear what I should do. I closed my eyes again and tried to push through my stupor. Nothing. Only a dull ache in my knee and the strange recollection of playing basketball. Had I played basketball? My eyes hurt too. I rubbed them with my right hand, felt the cuff of my sleeve on my face, and gave a jolt. My shirt, I was still dressed. Perhaps this girl and I had only slept together. I reached down hoping to feel my pants and belt. Nope, gone. I looked to my right and saw my slacks hanging from the back of a tall chair placed before a vanity mirror. I would have panicked, except that my head hurt too much. Well, I wasn't dressed for basketball. So how had I hurt my knee and what was I dressed for? Shirt, slacks—it wasn't work because I wasn't in Boston. I was dressed for a date. It was only then I realized that I wore the same thing to work that I wore on dates. Was there something in that? Was dating just another form of work? What was the point of a date? To meet a girl, fall in love, get married. It sounded a bit like work. And what was the point of marriage? Kids?

Suddenly my date with Jane materialized from the depths of my unconscious. The headache sharpened and the images emerged. Jane's black dress, The Columns Hotel, the bourbon—gag, though it was good bourbon—and her impending marriage to my brother. I paused on the unpleasantness of that particular portion of my recollection, hoping that by careful inspection I might discover that it was false, the result of too much drink. I rolled it around a bit, looked at it from all sides. No, ugly as it was, it was real. I tried to remember what

I had done about it, something clever I had said, some remarkable observation I had made to Jane that would change her mind or at least cast a shadow of absurdity upon the entire venture. No, nothing. I could recall no such comment. I desperately hoped that the comment was made. I was not optimistic.

My date with Jane had not been my finest hour, but there was something more there, lurking in the annals of my battered mind. Something in the idea of a date, that like the idea of bourbon now left me feeling sour. It was more than sour. It was a profound sense of humiliation, but it wasn't yet associated with anything in particular. Rather, it was a humiliation associated with the evening in general. I was confident that this feeling was key to understanding how I had arrived in this bed. I focused on it. And there it was: Milton, with those puppy dog eyes, trying to convince me to participate in his double date.

The rest of the evening came back in clumps, like curdled milk poured from the carton. Milton, the Paisano, those idiots from Arizona, The Mermaid, more Paisano, The Bombay Club, and swimming. We had gone swimming in the heated pool on the roof of The Royal Orleans Hotel, a marvelous pool overlooking the whole of the French Quarter. There we had passed the wee hours of the morning, drinking Paisano smuggled up by the Arizona brothers; Milton and the black brother on the observation deck staring into French Quarter hotel rooms through the coin-operated binoculars (they claimed to be monitoring the bourgeois culture for signs of capitalist perversion); the white brother and I in our boxer shorts in the pool with Milton's girlfriends.

Did the girls have bathing suits? I couldn't recall. I could remember the cool city breeze on my face, the warm water, the southern stars—different than those in Boston—and the sounds of the late crowd in the Quarter. Milton's girlfriends? I reflected on that idea for a moment. I turned and looked at the girl next to me. Holly? Or was it Rachel? Blonde, which was the blonde? Holly, yes, definitely. But how had I arrived in her bed? I couldn't remember how Milton had convinced me to participate in his dates, but surely he was to blame for my current sleeping arrangement. I had to get out of there.

I attempted to rescue my arm by pulling. I failed. Then I tried to roll her over. She was heavier in bed than she looked in a sweater and skirt. I pushed harder.

"Stop it, Milton," she growled.

This came as a bit of a blow. I didn't wish this accidental encounter to lead to something permanent, but neither did I wish that she forget me so quickly. I jerked my arm out from under her and crawled out of bed onto my sore knee. A spike of pain shot through my leg and up my spine, until it united with the dizzying headache that caused my vision to blur and signaled I was still drunk. The worst of my hangover was yet to come. This thought staggered me. What had I done to myself? Where was I?

Holly remained motionless; I presumed she was asleep. I pulled my pants back on, located my shoes, socks, and jacket. I couldn't find my watch or the golfer tie. I looked under the bed but discovered only a pile of photo albums. I stood up gingerly. My knee buckled, and a blinding pain shot through me again, following more or less the same path it had before, but this time settling squarely along the bridge of my nose. I squinted through it and tried harder to assess the situation. This was not a woman's apartment. It was a teenage girl's bedroom. I was in her home, her parents' home. There was a whole series of cheerleading photos on the wall above a dresser, on which sat two trophies and a teddy bear, and a collage of photos of girlfriends and boyfriends pinned to a corkboard above an immaculate desk. Everything in the room was in its place, except for me. I started to panic again but caught myself before hyperventilation set in.

Holly was still motionless. I limped to the window. No escape there. Jumping from the second story works well enough for action heroes, but I was no action hero. There were some azalea bushes below that might cushion the fall, but I could already imagine the double embarrassment of explaining to the paramedics why I had been in the girl's bedroom and why I had jumped from the window and broken my leg. One leg felt broken already. I tried the door.

The room opened onto a large indoor terrace over looking a magnificent foyer. It was obviously a grand house. There was a staircase at the end of the balcony. I closed the door behind me with a soft click and slowly walked toward the stairs, my shoes and jacket in my hands. I smelled coffee. Was it a flashback from yesterday's breakfast? Then I heard what were clearly ritual morning kitchen sounds: teaspoons stirring, newspapers rustling, a mother bustling about. It was real.

"Holly, are you up? We really must get going or else we'll be late."

I didn't answer.

"Holly?"

I knew then I was screwed. It was either the window or a bold walk out the front door during family breakfast. I stepped into a hallway bathroom and adjusted my clothes. I tucked in my shirt, put on my shoes and coat, and ran some water through my hair. If I was going to be caught sneaking out of the daughter's bedroom, better to be caught well dressed and presentable. I opened the door to the bathroom and tried to walk confidently down the stairs. I was still drunk enough to enjoy some of the artificial courage alcohol provided. As I stepped onto the main floor landing, I was relieved to discover that the entranceway offered no view of the dining room or kitchen. So far, I was unknown to the breakfast-eaters. I took a deep breath and strode across the hardwood floors, sights set on the door, a beautiful, ornate thing of glass and stained wood, ubiquitous in uptown New Orleans. I could barely believe that I was going to escape so easily. Through the glass I could see a porch, a few stairs, and a brick walkway leading across the grass to an iron gate set into a tremendous brick wall, and finally the street: freedom. I turned the doorknob and pulled. The door didn't move. I pushed. Still nothing. I pushed and pulled and began breathing somewhat erratically. I was trapped. Above the knob was a key-operated dead bolt. Such paranoia, typical New Orleans. For fire purposes, you were supposed to leave the key in the door when people were home. I felt like calling the fire marshal or, better yet, pretending to be the fire marshal and walking in on their breakfast to remind them of their life-threatening error. I gave up on the door. I looked around quickly. To the left was some type of parlor, a parlor with floor-to-ceiling windows. Why was that familiar? Had I been there before? I didn't have time to ponder it.

I stepped into the parlor, if that is what it was, and tried a window. It was an old wooden-framed job with tall panes of glass. The latch was pretty simple but, like the door, required a key, a key that was conspicuously absent. I looked about the room. Where did my mother keep her window keys? I noticed a tiny basket on the far bookshelf. Just the kind of place one would keep such things. I tiptoed over, opened the basket, pulled out a small set of keys, and returned to the window. There were two different types on the ring. One probably opened the windows and the other the heavy desk adjacent to the bookshelf. I tried the first version. It fit, but the lock didn't budge. I tried the second. It fit too, but again nothing.

"Goddamn, Milton," I whispered, trying to work the key. "Never leave uptown, something like this always happens." I could feel the alcohol-induced courage evaporating and with its departure the onset of a crippling hangover that made my hands tremble.

"What are you doing?" a small voice from behind asked. I whirled around. It was a child. He could not have been ten years old. I guess from the coat and slacks he figured I wasn't a burglar.

I curbed my urge to panic. "I'm trying to get this window open," I confessed. "Can you do it?" I offered him the keys.

He just stared at me.

I turned around and tried again with the first key. I pushed, pulled, stomped—and crash. Oops. The glass shattered. Then a deafening siren went off, followed by a megaphone voice reminiscent of those paranoid futuristic films of the '70s: "You have entered a secured area. The police have been notified. Leave immediately!" I guess I pushed, pulled, and stomped too hard. More sirens, more megaphone voice. The kid panicked and ran. I panicked but had nowhere to run. The windowpane was broken but not enough to crawl through. I started kicking out the rest of the glass to make my escape when I heard a new voice behind me.

"What the hell are you doing?"

It was an adult voice, but obviously startled by the alarm and the sight of a suit-wearing vandal kicking out his window from the inside.

I turned and saw what must have been Holly's father wearing a blue-and-white striped terry cloth robe. Despite my horror, I couldn't help but say "Good morning!" before I leaped through the broken window. I executed an acrobatic roll across the porch—a splendid Victorian wraparound with a handsome wooden railing. Ignoring my injured knee, I hurdled the railing, landing just beyond the azaleas that bordered the porch, and casually ran toward the gate. Everything about my escape was brilliant, except for the leisurely run.

Over the sound of the siren and megaphone voice, I heard the clenched growl of a dog. I turned just in time to see the toothy beast come racing around the corner of the house, directly at me. I shifted into a full sprint. Had the gate been unlocked, I would have had plenty of time.

It wasn't. I twisted the handle twice each way before I grabbed the top of the wrought iron and vaulted over. It was a tall gate, and with my knee feeling as it did, I was lucky to clear most of it. The short spikes caught the cuff of my pants and left a sizable tear below the knee, my sore knee.

Although the torn pants erased the possibility of a perfect escape, the proximity of Milton's car—and the fact that I didn't need a key to start it—was going to make up for a lot. In the spirit of James Bond, I rolled across the hood, opened the door, slipped into the driver's seat, and drove away in as much style as one can muster in a K-car: siren, megaphone voice, and barking dog fading in the background.

17

MY HEART WAS STILL POUNDING as I pulled up to my parents' home, a two-story New Orleans Gothic. Distracted by the heads-up display, I nearly hit the neighbor's Mercedes as he pulled out of his driveway. Mr. Robbins swerved and saved the day, but not without giving me a few choice words as he sped off to what was doubtless an early morning tee time. I didn't know that he had such a temper, and I hoped he didn't recognize me. After the near miss, I continued driving past my house, not wishing that he should return and see the K-car parked in front and realize that it was I who nearly killed him. I found a spot around the block on Palmer and threw the empty bottles of Paisano into the backseat. On the second toss, I heard a biological thump. It was the black brother still in his pink oxford and khaki pants, but now sporting a tweed overcoat and a gruesome twist across his face. The bottle hadn't been enough to stir him, so I gave him a gentle shake and began to say his name when I realized that I didn't know it. At this point, I balked. Without the protection of Milton's cool demeanor, I could not continue to call him "Arizona brother." Only Milton could get away with such a taciturn expression without causing offense. I was pretty sure he wasn't dead and figured he was safer in the back of the K-car than he would be in my parents' house. I might have chosen the K-car too, if given the choice.

Whatever moral advantage I felt after my recent escape was instantly lost when my sister Sarah opened the door before I could get the keys into the lock. She peered out from behind it cautiously, first looking around me as if afraid of something lurking outside. Then her eyes turned on me, the eyes of an insane interrogator, searching for guilt.

"I covered for you," she hissed, moving aside to let me in. She was wearing a blue satin, knee-length dress. Somewhat overdressed for Saturday morning, I thought.

"Covered what?"

"Your being out all night. I told Mom you left early this morning because you had errands to run."

"What time did you tell her I got up?"

"Six."

"On a Saturday morning? What the hell is she supposed to think I was doing? Delivering newspapers?"

"Well, what was I supposed to tell her? That you were out with one of your sluts?"

In conversations with my sisters, I often must remind myself that they are quite mad and usually confused. Unfortunately, in this case, Sarah's madness and probable confusion were uncomfortably close to the truth.

"Are you mad?" I asked flatly.

"Don't start that with me this morning. I can't believe I bothered to cover for you. What with the way you treat me—"

"Thanks," I interrupted. "Whereas before I would have told Mother I was out all night, now I must develop some elaborate lie explaining where I went at six this morning."

"Where were you off to this morning?" My mother's voice emerged from nowhere, a voice that could shatter glass at ten paces. Fortunately, I had lost my watch, thus saving its expensive crystal face. The rest of her then appeared. "Thank God you are back. I thought you had forgotten about brunch. I can't imagine what you had to do. What is open at six on Saturday?"

There was silence. I looked at Sarah. Sarah glared at me for a moment before she turned and sulked her way up the stairs. I turned to my mother.

"Good morning, Mother," I said, hoping to deflect the questions about my morning. I failed.

"What have you been doing? I needed you this morning. Everyone thinks I can do everything around here myself."

I just stared at her, bleary-eyed.

"I needed you to pick up your aunt at the airport."

I was starting to fade out of the conversation at this point. Dear as she was, conversations with my mother tended to be one-sided. I knew trying to organize our family was no mean feat, but after the night I'd had, I simply couldn't keep up with her. She mentioned something about my aunt's plane being late and the need for us to leave anyway.

"I don't know what we are going to do about your aunt. Leave a note on the door?"

Without the vaguest idea what she was talking about, it was easy for me to agree with her that I didn't know what to do either.

"Well, at least you are dressed, and thank God for that because we must leave in five minutes."

"Where are we going?" I asked, amazed at the thought of going out rather than directly to bed as I had planned.

"Why, to brunch at Commander's. We cannot be late. We are meeting the other families."

My mother had never believed in the fashion of lateness, and she stormed off to round up the rest of our family. I could hear feet crashing about upstairs in response to her shouts. I staggered into the kitchen in search of a restorative. I remembered a college girlfriend who insisted that eating an apple was equivalent to thirty minutes of sleep, a cold shower to a full hour, and something about ice cream and coffee. I couldn't recall exactly, but as I didn't have time for a shower and I could see no apples laid out, I grabbed the K&B vanilla ice cream out of the freezer, scooped it into a bowl, added what was left of the coffee, and sprinkled ibuprofen over the top to give it some crunch. The chill of the ice cream provided some relief to the headache that had spread halfway down my back. I was still eating and making an oath never to drink again when Tabatha's date arrived.

Despite my constant immersion in the city's culture, I had never really understood the debutante ritual, an endless stream of parties, teas, lunches, brunches, and social calls, all for the purpose of making the girl officially available for social life and marriage. Of course, my sister hadn't waited for her debut to kick off her social life. But even a socialite like Tabatha needed a little help in the dating department during her debut. Debutantes typically require different dates for all official events, and as there are so many, the debutante needs a lengthy list of prospective escorts. Consequently, the gentlemen are rarely of any romantic significance, often chosen for the sake of convenience. For this brunch, my mother had selected my cousin James as Tabatha's companion.

James was shy and looked out of place in his pin-striped suit, probably borrowed for this occasion. He was instructed by my mother to sit on the couch and wait; we would be leaving in five minutes. I joined him in the living room and offered him some ice cream and coffee, but he confessed that the suit was his father's and he dared not soil it. I wondered how he planned to get through brunch. Fortunately, these required dates were not required to perform. He would have to eat something, in order to avoid appearing morose, but he would be allowed to sit through brunch without saying anything more than "How do you do?" and "Very nice to meet you." Based on what I saw, James looked perfect for that part. When ten minutes had passed and it became clear that our departure was not imminent, James relaxed and mentioned Sunday's Saints game. I was in no mood for small talk, but James was too nervous to remain quiet in my presence, so I went along with him. He explained that the Saints were losing, but there remained a mathematical possibility they could make the playoffs. He expounded on this in painful detail. The situation was fairly typical for the Saints. They would need to win the remainder of their games, which at this point was equal to the number of games they had won all year. Furthermore, every other NFC team would need to lose the remainder of their nonconference games, except for the first-place teams in each NFC division, which would need to win the remainder of their games, except those they played against the Saints. I knew all of this already, having kept up with the Saints religiously. I had tried to follow Boston sports, but they were too good for my New Orleans sensibilities. The Boston teams had all enjoyed dynastic periods and were always competitive. On more than one occasion, I had wondered if my failure to embrace the Patriots or the Celtics was out of loyalty to the New Orleans franchises or rather a more general commitment on my part to mediocrity. New Orleans sports teams might enjoy brief moments of success, but such success always felt like an anomaly.

I had convinced myself that it was loyalty, but loyalty to what? What is loyalty to a sports team? Is it loyalty to the owner, the billionaire who owns and operates the organization for personal profit? Is it loyalty to the players, millionaires who change teams regularly and show less loyalty to the team that pays them than I am expected to show for the team I pay to watch? And what of those players? Why should I care for their performance? Do I know them? They expect me to celebrate their victories, but do they celebrate mine? Do they follow the ups and downs of my career? It is a codependent relationship.

"Is there any chance of this happening, James?" I asked, bringing my internal critique of professional football to an end.

James began some form of explanation. "Well, if . . ." and then he saw I wasn't buying it and admitted no. I rose from the couch and limped into the kitchen in search of something to combat the alcohol-induced dehydration that was causing my fingers to clench. "But I still have hope," he said, just loud enough for me to hear him from the living room.

This is the secret of despair—that it confronts absurdity and attempts to negotiate with it. German and French philosophers had written countless chapters trying to explain the obscure nature of despair, but had they been sports enthusiasts, they might have come to the crux of the matter more easily. On the other hand, if they were enthusiastic for New Orleans sports, they might not have seen this despair as anything out of the ordinary.

I returned with a pitcher of orange juice and two glasses tucked under my arm. I thought orange juice might relieve James' despair, but he declined the refreshment before I had an opportunity to offer. So I handed him the two empty glasses, sat down, and began drinking the orange juice directly from the pitcher.

With his Saints fantasy destroyed and his despair fully engaged, James turned to the subject of work. He was unemployed and fearful that somebody at brunch might ask him what he did. I suggested that he say he smoked, but he found no humor in this. His aunt had told him it was acceptable for him to say he was between jobs. I laughed at this stratagem and told him to put the empty glasses on the coffee table. He did as told and then asked if I would put in a good word with our uncle in Boston. He said he was willing to move, but more importantly, what he wanted was the ability to say, with some degree of truth, that he was considering moving to Boston for work. I gulped more of the orange juice and told him that the work was wretched but that I would be happy to vouch for him, or merely go along with his ruse, if he preferred. I assured him there was no reason to take a crappy job in Boston to save face at a debutante brunch.

My mother's five minutes was as much a fantasy as James' playoff-bound Saints, though the fault lay entirely with my sisters. The shouting from upstairs was continual. The girls could be heard complaining, critiquing, and crying in equal proportion to my mother's berating them for their tardiness and puerile fashion sense. As it turned out, I could have napped, showered, changed, and walked to the market to buy an apple. Instead, I frittered away nearly an hour talking nonsense to James before the family was finally herded into cars, en route to Commander's Palace. I tossed back a second round of ibuprofen, finished the orange juice, and limped to the car, carefully staring at the horizon the way a dancer does in order to stop my head from spinning. Everything on my body ached from the swelling hangover, matched only by my swelling knee. As I climbed slowly into the passenger's seat of my father's new Buick, I prayed that the orange juice, coffee, ice cream, and ibuprofen would opt to remain in my body made uninhabitable by alcohol, rather than find new residence on the car's comfortable leather interior. Because it was brunch, there was a lingering chance that I could be home and in bed by noon, and that thought alone sustained me.

18

THE SUGAR-AND-CAFFEINE BUZZ failed to improve my mood or the company, but the brunch was splendid. It was a typical Commander's Palace affair: beginning with turtle soup, oven-roasted oysters, eggs Sardou, shrimp rémoulade, jazz music, and a steady supply of sparkling wines, cocktails, and tea to balance the hors d'oeuvres and conversation. My father had reserved a huge table, large enough to seat our entire family and those of the two debutantes hosting that evening's ball with my sister.

Tabatha was not, by her nature, a sophisticated woman. An evening out for her was more likely to include crashing a fraternity party and drinking beer from a funnel than attending the New Orleans symphony or going to a coffee shop for insightful exchange. But here at Commander's, she was perfectly at ease, drinking tea and guiding what little talk there was like a professional. As the various guests arrived, she would join my mother in welcoming them. Either she had been well coached by our mother, or like Henry V, she had been concealing her noble nature until her coming out.

Unfortunately, this brunch was a union of convenience. The three families occupied the same social circles, knew the same people, attended the same functions, and were all members of the New Orleans Country Club, but I had never previously met the Trenchards or the Calloways. This brunch, along with all the other affairs, was held together solely by the common bond of the debut. Despite Tabatha's efforts, the union of these families did not prove to be particularly stimulating.

The conversation began with the arrival of Mr. and Mrs. Trenchard and their very homely daughter Elizabeth, wearing something pink that highlighted her blotchy complexion, meager bosom, and her date. Then came compliments on the debutantes' dresses. Each debutante paid the other a simple "I love that dress," and each mother a more sophisticated "Where did you find such a wonderful outfit?" Gradually, the small talk moved to the dresses they would wear that evening, the dresses that had been worn in years past, and the dresses that should never have been worn at all. I found it all mind-numbingly tedious, which in my state was not entirely unwelcome, but I knew that a discussion of women's clothing could be particularly treacherous, with the slightest misstep risking anger and tears. Equally sensitive to this peril, the husbands wisely kept to the milk punch cocktails, shrimp, and oysters that arrived on large silver platters. I believe Mr. Trenchard mentioned the Saints once, but his wife cast him a quick frown of disapproval and the subject was dropped. Apparently, football was not a suitable topic for a debutante brunch. I worried for James.

Though the Calloways were still absent, after two rounds of drinks the delay could no longer be endured, and we were seated. It was not entirely uncommon for guests to arrive late at these affairs, or depart early, given the multitude of social engagements this time of year, but it was odd that one of the debutantes and her parents should be so tardy. I was placed between Mr. Trenchard and Sarah, so I directed my attention to Mr. Trenchard, who, with the delivery of a third milk punch, braved the waters of conversation again and asked quietly if I did any sailing in Boston. I confessed that I had crewed a few times for a girlfriend's father but that the very strict code against drinking while racing had taken some of the fun out of it for me. It wasn't so much the lack of alcohol that bothered me as knowing that the absence of it was based on a strong sense of principle. I never cared for strong principles of any kind, but they seemed particularly ill-suited to leisure activities designed to relieve us of the burdens of our caste and station. Trenchard failed to see my point and proudly announced that he never allowed drinking on his boat before the start of a race.

"Too much traffic at the start, you know, liable to hit someone if you are fooling around with your beer."

Although I agreed, I felt it unnecessary to say so. He wasn't really asking.

The bartender was making the milk punch with brandy instead of bourbon, the scent of which had a soothing effect on my constitution. I wasn't drinking mine, but I could smell it on Trenchard's breath as he regaled me with his nautical tales. He looked over his shoulder at his wife to make sure he had sea room and then launched into a brandy-flavored account of his most recent yachting victory: first in class in the New Orleans to Gulfport regatta. He finished his third milk punch and ordered another by the time he had reached the first mark. I leaned back and prepared for a lengthy retelling of the race. I was not disappointed. Through the steady stream of new arrivals, aunts and uncles, cousins, nephews and nieces, I listened to Trenchard's tales of the sea and ate delicately fried strips of eggplant dusted with Parmesan cheese. Introductions were made all around, but Trenchard and I merely nodded at the names as he narrated his heroic tacking duel through the Rigolets. As Trenchard's boat reached the drawbridge that leads into Lake Borgne, which is no lake at all but rather a bay, Jane walked in, alone, in a close-fitting, black-and-white striped dress that made her look like an Italian sports car or a football referee, the metaphor was unclear. Was she here to see me? Why? The bridge opened for Trenchard's boat. I stood up to greet Jane.

Jane only glanced at me in passing and walked over to my sister Tabatha, who welcomed her and made the appropriate introductions. She left me out. Jane then sat at the far end of the table, so far that I could only see her nose and chin and the drink she lifted occasionally. She was drinking juice, leaving me to wonder if she had chosen to drink juice rather than the cocktails and wines that were being offered because she was pregnant. She seemed tense and refused to look in my direction. Her social skills were impeccable, but I could tell that her manner was forced. Why was she so nervous? That was the real question. Was it because she was going to be announcing her engagement to my brother in front of all these people that very night? Was it because she still loved me and couldn't acknowledge me without revealing her overwhelming desire? I laughed out loud, which surprised Trenchard, who was describing a rather tedious passage through the barrier islands. Jane must have been anxious about the engagement. Who wouldn't be when marrying into this brood?

Before I had gotten comfortable with Jane's presence, William arrived, the bastard. He waltzed around the room, shaking everyone's hand and offering a grotesque peck of a kiss to each of the women, including Jane. The grandmothers loved him. The debutantes endured him only for the sake of form. He sat down at the opposite end of the table from Jane, showing her no particular attention.

He explained why he was late, though it was utterly unnecessary as other guests were still arriving. He had driven his new car, some German thing, and he would not allow the valet to park it. This was foolish of him, since he had to buy the new German car to replace the previous one he had totaled. The car had a better chance with the valet driving it. He tasted the sparkling wine my father had chosen for the brunch, Montaudon, and then in a voice that could be heard in the next parish asked the waitress to bring him a bottle of Chateau de something or other. William was very proud of his voice and regularly described it as booming and operatic. Everyone I knew just thought it was loud.

"Make it two bottles, in case there is another con-noisseur among us," he added with a wink—a wink that declared to all the other pompous men in the room, "I am one of you. Oh quite. No doubt."

I felt nauseated. There were too many candidates for the cause to be sure, between listening to my brother, watching Jane, and the tremendous volume of spirits I had consumed the night before. But when I contemplated each, my stomach heaved the most with the sound of William's voice.

He appeared particularly pleased with himself and went on to order a special bowl of soup. I couldn't hear what he wanted because Trenchard was delivering an animated account of his finish, but the house turtle soup would not satisfy William this morning.

"And a glass of water," even though he already had one, "and make sure that everyone else has a glass of water too, please."

I wanted to throw my water at him, but without warning, he looked my way and said, "Brother, how are you this morning? I trust you are feeling better than you were last night."

"Splendid. Excuse me." I stood up and limped to the toilet. I know that this move played right into William's suggestion that I had been drunk and was now hungover, but I couldn't stand to listen to him any longer. Better to concede that point than slug it out over an unbecoming, effort at wit. Unbecoming for both of us. If his wit succeeded, I would be the butt of it. If it failed, I would be linked to it by our fraternity.

"Nice pants," he boomed as I limped away, unsure whether he was speaking to me or another guest.

In the restroom, I washed my face and hands and combed my hair with still wet fingers. I stared hard at the mirror. What was I to do? I couldn't go back out there. On one side, I had Jane ignoring me; on the other, I had my brother trying to engage me in conversation. I couldn't just leave, not without an excuse. I searched my mind for some kind of pretext. Nothing there. Damn.

I tried to collect myself. I didn't look too bad. I stepped back from the mirror to get a full view. Oh God, my pants. The tear was as plain as the Paisano stain that surrounded it and made it look as though I had been stabbed. How had I forgotten? Why had nobody noticed? Of course, the women were too busy paying attention to Tabatha's attire to observe I was walking around Commander's Palace with shark-bitten slacks. James was too busy worrying about his unemployment, but my brother spotted it. I wondered if I could use the torn slacks as an excuse to leave. "Mom, I tore my slacks in the restroom and must return home." I imagined her response. She would gasp, turn to me embarrassed, and ask, "What were you doing in the restroom?" No, I couldn't have that. I would simply have to return to the brunch, torn pants and all. Hoping to gain courage and refreshment from the water, I washed my face again. There wasn't much courage there, but I was reminded how desperately dehydrated I was. I bent over the sink and drank directly from the faucet.

"Excuse me, sir, are you OK?" a mystery voice came seemingly from nowhere. Startled, I jumped and hit my lip against the metal spigot.

It was a waiter. "Yes, fine thanks," I said, but could feel my lip beginning to bleed.

"I'm sorry to have frightened you. Are you certain you're OK? A lady at your table asked me to come check on you."

Jane, could it have been Jane? Probably my mother.

"I am fine, thanks again."

I stepped past him into the hall and limped back to the dining room. I reminded myself that brunch could not last forever and that after brunch I would reward my patience with a long, much needed nap. As I approached the table, I saw Holly standing next to my sister. I stopped dead, stared, then shamelessly hid behind a large indoor palm decorating the entrance. With Holly were faces I had seen: her little brother and her father, now out of his blue-and-white striped terry cloth robe and in a blue sport coat and slacks. Clasping his arm was a forty-year-old version of Holly in a light-blue dress, and the older gentleman in a dark gray suit was probably a relative functioning as her date.

After my sister performed the usual social graces, Holly's father apologized for his family's lateness and explained that their house had been broken into that very morning. Everyone at the table was shocked. Holly's father was still obviously distraught. He said that the worst part was dealing with the police.

"The police do nothing. They write reports for insurance claims and drive away. They make no effort to catch these villains. The police refused to dust for prints or collect DNA evidence. No wonder criminals roam the streets with impunity."

Everyone at the table agreed. I felt like an idiot. I looked at Holly. She was standing there, staring at the floor, trying to ignore everything. She obviously hadn't told her father the truth and now felt like an idiot too.

The wife piped in. "Nothing was taken that we know of, but you feel so violated—somebody breaking into your home while you are there. It's very upsetting."

Expressions of shock and nods circled the table, with someone commenting about it being the principle of the thing. My brother added that these criminals should all be hunted down and shot.

Holly's father spoke up again. "Well, I won't let this happen to me without a fight. I want justice. I called a private detective agency. They're sending somebody out this afternoon."

I felt my lip bleeding. Holly's family took their various places, and her father was asked to recount the details of the event again. I ran back to the restroom and washed my face again.

After the second handful of water, I realized I was not actually in any great danger of going to prison. Surely Holly would confess that I was her guest before she would allow me to go to jail for breaking out of her house. But I couldn't return to the brunch. If I did, her father and brother would recognize me. I didn't have an alibi now that Sarah had told the family I had gone out at six that morning. Either Holly would have to admit that we had slept together, which would destroy her entire debut, or she would remain silent, in which case I would be carted off in handcuffs and accused of all sorts of depravity by family and friends. Either way, it was going to be an ugly scene. I simply had to leave.

I wasn't thinking clearly, but you can't force clarity, especially not on the hangover I was battling. I washed my face once more, and the sink filled with blood from my split lip.

"You look like hell," Milton said, standing over me with a towel. I wasn't surprised. Nothing could surprise me any longer. "What happened to your lip and your pants?"

"The waiter did it."

"Nice. And this is supposed to be a classy joint."

"What are you doing here?" I asked, taking the paper towel and applying it to my face.

"I am looking for my brother. I have reason to believe you stole him, along with my car."

"Yeah, I have them both. They're at my parents' house. How did you find me here?"

"I have a friend who works here. Maybe the one who bloodied your lip? Anyway, I described you, and he said he had seen you hobble into the restroom."

I was confused. "No, I mean, how did you know I was at Commander's Palace? And why am I limping? Did we play basketball?"

"We did not play basketball. You are limping because you jumped out of a second-story window. As for my knowing your whereabouts, well, it is a long, dismal story that involves you stabbing me in the back and stealing my girlfriend. But I will give you the short version. I called Holly's house looking for my car, and she said that you had it. So I walked to your house, but the car was not there. I knocked on your door and found nobody home. There was, however, a note. A note for your Aunt Dee that she should meet the family at Commander's Palace. So I got on the streetcar and came down here." He paused with a degree of seriousness.

"I would like my car and my brother back. I have important business this afternoon that requires both."

"I fell out of a window?" I was a bit dumbfounded by the suggestion. I was also wondering what Milton meant exactly when he said I had stolen his girlfriend. That I simply absconded with her, the way I had taken his car and his black brother, or did he know that I had slept with her? I decided to leave that subject for another time, perhaps never.

"Not fell, jumped. You jumped out of the second-story window of Stefan's apartment."

Stefan, the naked roommate, the crowded dance party, the disco light, it all came back to me like a hangover with a second wind.

Milton continued, "It is amazing you weren't hurt."

"I was hurt. I can barely walk," I pointed out.

"Oh please. You were dancing in the streets with Holly afterward. God knows what you did to her after you dropped us off," he said sharply.

"I drove home?"

"You insisted. Insisted you were the only sober one among us. No one was prepared to argue with you. I fell asleep on the way and woke up on my front porch with an Arizona brother next to me. I don't have any idea what happened to Rachel. Do you?"

I had no idea. "I believe I let her off at her house," I lied unconvincingly. "Have you spoken with her?"

"Not yet. I have been busy trying to track down my brother and my car, or perhaps you forgot."

"I parked your car on Palmer Street."

"Why Palmer Street?" Then his expression changed. "You Boston, fucking elitist. You were embarrassed to park a K-car in front of your house. Son of a bitch!"

I explained that it wasn't elitism but rather the heads-up display that nearly put me into the backseat of the neighbor's Mercedes. And Palmer Street didn't require parallel parking. Milton accepted my explanation and acknowledged that his aftermarket addition took some getting used to.

"I have a bigger problem than your K-car."

"Bigger than a fat lip and torn slacks?"

"Much. I must figure a way to escape this brunch."

"Just leave. I can't imagine your conversation will be missed."

"First, I can't leave without saying good-bye. My mother would kill me."

"So say good-bye and leave."

"That's where it gets complicated. I cannot be seen by . . ." I hesitated. Should I just tell Milton the truth about Holly and me? Had he already figured it out? I decided to lie. "Jane."

"Oh God. Isn't this a bit tired? Jane, Jane, Jane. All you ever talk about is Jane."

At this point, another restaurant patron entered the restroom. The sound he produced while conducting his business instantly underscored how inappropriate this environment was for our scheming. It also made clear that Holly's father could join us at any moment. I decided to bring things to a close.

"Can you help me?" I asked.

"How?"

In a pinch, Milton could be a man of few words, and I imagined he sensed the urgency in my voice.

"Can you pass on my regrets to the brunchers and explain that an urgent matter arose that I could not put off?"

"Sure. In this case, do you believe it better if I make up an urgent matter or leave that to the imagination?"

I shuddered at the thought of Milton making up an excuse for me. "Oh no. Just leave it vague."

"Indeed, always the best policy. First rule of deceit: Do no harm."

"Just so. Mention that I had to leave, that I am fine, and express my regrets to my mother and the debutantes."

"Debutantes?" Milton asked in a hushed shout. "You didn't tell me this was a debutante occasion."

"It is. A debutante brunch."

"I should have guessed, I suppose, but I was distracted."

"Distracted?"

"I had two dates last night," he explained. "It taxed me."

"I know," I said with as much sarcasm as I could muster.

"Please. There you were last night, standing high on your moral soapbox, condemning my dating practices, and here you are in full pursuit of a passel of debutantes yourself. I am impressed at your duplicity."

I began to speak, but Milton silenced me with a wave. He looked as if he'd had an epiphany.

"That is why you cannot be seen by Jane. You brutalize all those socialites and then she catches you at a debutante brunch."

I started to resist but concluded that this explanation was safer than the truth. "Just do it. And try not to make a scene."

"I can't believe I wasn't invited."

"What?"

"I can't believe I wasn't invited. I know your family."

"I wouldn't worry. This was just a family event. The three families throwing the ball aren't very close. The brunch is a social sleight of hand, affording them the opportunity to get to know one another better so that tonight they might give the appearance of being dear friends."

"Sure, but I still should have been invited, especially if . . ." Milton obviously intended to say more but, for once, stopped himself. As far as I was concerned, it was a promising change. I wanted to leave the restroom and the restaurant as soon as possible.

"OK. I put it in your capable hands. How are you getting home?"

"Streetcar, unless you have a better suggestion."

"We can ride together. I'll meet you on St. Charles."

"Have you the fare?"

"You spent my cash last night."

"I'll find more."

"No doubt." I paused a moment. "Well, good luck."

Milton grinned with profound self-assurance. I considered mentioning that Holly and her family were part of the group, merely out of concern for myself: If Milton was distracted by their presence, he may fail to execute a satisfactory apology for my absence. There was no point in hiding it from him, as he would come to know the truth very soon, but I didn't know how to bring it up. He had already halfheartedly accused me of stealing his girlfriend. How could I say it smartly and vitiate the injury to Milton? Milton preferred a well-formed sentence to a well-formed girlfriend, so I decided to place more confidence in Milton's ability to cope with this unexpected development than my ability to explain it. The first rule of deceit: Do no harm.

Milton gave me a meager bow and exited. I waited a moment and then followed him at a distance. I was desperate to know how he would pull this off and fearful that by allowing him to help me I may have opened a Pandora's box. I hid around the corner, out of sight but within earshot of the proceedings.

"Ladies and gentlemen," he began simply. It got complicated quickly.

"Milton?" I heard Tabatha and Holly ask simultaneously.

"Tabatha? Holly? How, uh, delightful to see you."

THE BASKETBALL GAME

The closest thing we have to the traditional
ideology of the leisure class is a group of
artists and intellectuals who regard their
work as play and their play as work.

David Riesman

ANTIPASTO DI ROBERTO

½ LB SLICED ASIAGO
½ LB SLICED PECORINO ROMANO
½ LB SLICED PROSCIUTTO DI PARMA
½ LB SLICED PARMIGIANO-REGGIANO
½ LB SLICED CACCIATORINI DI CINGHIALE
¼ LB SLICED ARTICHOKE HEARTS
¼ LB GREEN OLIVES
¼ LB BLACK OLIVES
¼ LB ROASTED RED PEPPERS

Serve on a large wooden platter
with olive oil.

19

"**Y**OU MUST ADMIT it was a brilliant recovery."

Milton leaned back into the tired, brown couch that showed the scars of many a Mardi Gras. Before him was a heavy coffee table with a pitcher of water, two beer mugs, and an array of empty beer cans.

"Brilliant insofar as it saved my ass and brilliant insofar as it will be the talk of the town for years, but not so brilliant for a man wanted by the police for fraud."

"You might have warned me that Holly and her family were there. You can imagine my surprise. It was no small feat of social acrobatics to navigate that terrain. And how was I to know that your brother was with the police?"

"He's not a cop. He works for the district attorney."

"Same thing," snorted Milton.

"Only if you're wanted for stealing from banks."

"I did not steal any money. I merely borrowed it at eighteen percent annual interest, compounded monthly."

"The name on the credit card was Milton Sincerely. Are you Milton Sincerely?"

"No, that is my credit card name. It keeps my creditors at bay," Milton said, slumping even further into the worn cushions. "It also has a pleasant ring, don't you think? And it is the perfect cover. Who would expect a man named 'Sincerely' of working to overthrow the capitalist empire?"

"Or of paying for a debutante brunch with a fraudulent credit card?"

"I didn't offer to pay for the entire brunch, merely a round of drinks."

Milton had managed the whole thing gracefully enough. He arranged it with a waiter in advance, so that once he announced my untimely exit, the waiter would arrive with a bill for the drinks already rung up and paid. This was designed to deflect questions about the nature of my emergency.

It had gone off almost flawlessly. Milton first begged to be pardoned for interrupting the brunch and offered to buy a round. In accord with the efficiency that distinguishes the service at Commander's Palace, the waiter appeared right on cue: "The drinks you ordered for the ladies and gentlemen, Mr. Sincerely," he had said in a professionally bored voice. What Milton had not counted on was the waiter calling him by the name on his card.

"Sincerely?" asked Tabatha. She knew him as Sawyer.

Seeing his carefully crafted departure unraveling, he signed the statement quickly, snapped his heels with the greatest drama he could muster, turned, and left. But William was on to him.

"Sincerely? Milton Sincerely?" William muttered to himself for some time. William was not quick-witted.

Then with everything his operatic voice could summon, "That credit card's no good. He's a fraud!"

But his epiphany had come a moment too late. Milton was gone.

"The funny bit is that my father fought for you like a lion," I said. "He kept insisting that such a well-spoken and well-dressed man, 'not like the ragtag degenerates that are so common these days,' couldn't possibly be a petty thief."

"I can't believe you were lurking in the shadows just to witness the aftermath. You are shameless, though I am pleased to hear that I have a fan club. I always liked your father."

"He won't be such a fan when he discovers that you've been arrested for borrowing money with no intention of repaying it. Even in California, they call that fraud."

"At eighteen percent," Milton leaned forward and poured water from the pitcher into one of the beer mugs. "Eighteen percent, it's, it's infamous." He took a sip of water and continued. "It is usury, you know. There was a time when people who charged such a rate would be run out of town or put in the stockade. Now it is simply called clever marketing, but they are still criminals, usurers. I have employed their criminal credit card in protest of their wanton disregard for all standards of human decency." He was raving.

"They are criminals, you know. Read your Bible. Whom do they think they are fooling? They will certainly be the first ones with their backs against the wall when the revolution comes. Anyway, that credit card was good. Your brother's concern would have come to nothing."

He drained the beer mug of its contents and poured it full again. "William will get his comeuppance like the rest of them."

"Are you finished?"

"Yes."

"Excellent. I hope you'll refrain from any further cavalier displays of wealth. Most of the folks who know you know you're a graduate student. An unemployed graduate student."

"They let me teach a class."

"Indeed, a more or less unemployed graduate student who uses his philosophy class as a dating service while defrauding the nation's banks."

"Here's wishing them a speedy demise," raising his mug of water and drinking all of it again.

"But they fund your lifestyle," I said, leaning over to the coffee table and topping up both mugs.

"That's exactly why I hate them. Look what I have become," he raised his arms referring to the apartment's decor: late twentieth century, unwanted, and appropriated from the side of the road. In addition to the ancient couch, the spacious living room boasted a reclining chair that looked like it had been dragged behind a truck. It was permanently fixed in the reclined position and bent so that the footrest did not line up with the seat. There also was an old, cabinet-style TV that we had rescued from salvage years ago. The thing must have weighed three hundred pounds, requiring five of us to move it into the apartment. Now there was another TV on top of the cabinet TV. Milton had pointed to it and described it as "picture in picture." Next to the TVs was a bookshelf housing a stereo, record player, tape player, and two rows of well-worn science fiction novels. Two identical prints in identical frames graced either side of an archway that separated the living room and dining room. Opposite Milton's couch was an old wingback chair, which was where I now sat. The coffee table that pulled the room together sat upon an old rug that seemed to be the source for a fragrance that hinted at wet socks, perhaps stale beer, perhaps both. The smell and furnishings, juxtaposed with the stark white walls, twelve-foot ceilings, and hardwood floors, created a shabby, minimalist ambiance that was calming and comforting.

"I am a materialist, a shameless materialist. And I want more."

"More of this?" I cast a doubtful eye upon the recliner.

"Well, I wouldn't mind leather."

"All the better to seduce your eighteen-year-olds."

"Watch it. I saved your ass today. You owe me a little gratitude."

"You're right," I admitted freely. I did owe him. "You saved me from that band of brunching ruffians. They were monsters, monsters in dresses, sport coats, and slacks. All sitting around that oversized conglomeration of tables, devouring whatever food and drink came within reach, and talking a mile a minute about nothing at all."

"Sounds perfectly pleasant to me."

"And Jane was there with my brother."

"Is that jealousy I detect? Surely you are over Jane by now. It has been nearly twenty-four hours."

I ignored him and went on. "And William, that ass, sits halfway across the room from Jane, as if he didn't know her, and flirts with one of the waitresses."

"The cad." He lifted his beer mug and finished it off in one extended slurp. "Sounds like a pretty typical debutante brunch." He sighed deeply and placed the mug on the table. "I only wish I had been invited."

"Apparently you were."

"What?"

This really surprised him, and I could see the hurt in his eyes. A missed opportunity to monitor the bourgeoisie in action, to flirt with the bourgeois daughters.

"I was invited? Why wasn't I informed?" Milton stood up. "Why didn't you tell me?"

"I didn't know," I hedged, though I was enjoying the taunt. In fact, I hadn't known and still wasn't sure, but from the scene that had unfolded upon Milton's arrival at the table, something very devious was afoot. I would have to bluff Milton to test my hypothesis. "And why didn't you tell me about your affair with my sister?" I asked, lifting an empty, green beer bottle next to me and waving it at him.

"Your sister? What on earth are you talking about?"

"You know precisely what I am talking about. It was she who invited you. I don't know why you didn't get the invitation. I assure you I had nothing to do with it."

"What?" Milton was surprised again. I loved to surprise him. It was very rare.

"Well, it's only a theory."

"Go on."

"I have only a casual acquaintance with how these debutante affairs operate, but it seems that my sister invited you or asked someone else to invite you. Perhaps she asked my aunt to recommend you to my mother. Again, I have no notion of the proper procedure for invitations. But I know that there is a procedure, and my sister was somehow thwarted, because when it was evident that all of her guests had arrived, she became very agitated." I would need to lie to carry my charade the distance. "Eventually, she conjured up the courage to ask me if you were coming."

"What did you say?"

More lies. "Naturally, I said I had no idea. I told her that I didn't know you were invited but foolishly added that I didn't think that you knew. At that point, all the female eyes looked up at once and a hush fell over the table. It was obvious that a coup of some form had occurred and prevented your attendance. Of course, as polite society requires, my sister should have changed the subject at that moment, and as the most rational of all my siblings, I fully expected her to do so." The lie was getting quite interesting, so I ran with it. "She's a flake like my other sister, but she is perfectly aware of her social responsibilities. She failed herself. She became distraught, looking about, seeking out the guilty party among all of us present. The men all looked down or hid behind their cocktails. The women traded glances of suspicion. The moment was really very tense. And that's how I knew there was something between you two."

"What?" Milton feigned innocence, retrieving his empty mug from the table. But I knew something was up. I didn't know the details yet, but Milton had given away too much.

"She would not have lost hold of herself in such a way had it been just anyone missing from her party, so I knew it must be a gentleman."

"Well, I am a very fetching addition to any gathering. Surely you can understand that your sister, or any discriminating hostess, would feel more disappointed at my absence than your average witless party drone." He toyed with the empty beer mug.

"Witless party drone indeed. I presume you are referring to me."

"I am."

"Flattery will get you nowhere."

"It did with your sister," Milton laughed.

I frowned.

"I'm just joking," he defended.

"But I know it's true." I paused to read his expression, but he remained calm. "You proved last night that you are not above pursuing young, defenseless girls." Milton made as if to protest, but I stopped him with a wave of the hand. "What amazes me is that you would have time, given your obviously busy social schedule, to pursue a third . . . and that number three should be my sister."

"Please don't take it as a slight to your sister. She's a lovely girl. I am quite taken with her. I might even say that I love her."

"Love?" I gasped. "So I was right? You are having an affair with my sister!" I leaped to my feet in anger, but the anger wasn't there. It was shock: I was surprised to discover I was correct. My instincts were rarely correct. Even as the shock dissipated, the rage I was expected to feel failed to appear. In part because I was as guilty as Milton, in part because I never liked the other guys Tabatha chose to love, and in part because it was Milton. But mostly because I was so proud of my powers of ratiocination. I sat back down and traded the discarded beer bottle for a mug and drank as much water as possible in a few swallows. Though almost religiously disingenuous, Milton had been genuinely surprised that he wasn't invited to the party, which meant that he believed one of the girls owed him an invitation. Elizabeth was too homely for his taste, and he had already indicated his awareness that Holly— or was it Rachel?—had a debutante event this weekend that he was skipping. That only left my sister Tabatha as the source of his disappointment.

"Why not? Is it so hard to believe?" Milton asked.

"Yes. Of course it is. You were out with two other girls last night. If you truly love my sister," I stuttered, "Christ, I can barely say it. If you, you, well you know."

"Know what? You're not making any sense."

"How can you be with two other girls when you claim to love a third?"

"I don't follow you."

"How can you be with Holly and Rachel when you love Tabatha?"

The problem here was that I knew I was a hypocrite. I sounded less like someone making an accusation and more like someone hoping to be convinced. Milton wasn't very convincing.

"I compartmentalize."

Milton got up to refill the pitcher.

"You're a womanizer," I shouted at him as he fumbled in the kitchen. "A womanizer who takes advantage of girls instead of women," I asserted, unsatisfied with his explanation.

"Of course I am, and, yes, I do," he said, returning now with two pitchers of water. "That's why girls love me." I leaned back into the battered wingback chair and waited for the rest of the story. "If I am liberal with my affections, women don't mind so much. They prefer a man who loves women to one who loves his work or his hobbies. At least they know I care about women. Why do you think battered women stay with the men who batter them so often? At least a man who beats them thinks about them, cares about them, even if his caring is cruel."

We had dispensed with the beer mugs and were now drinking directly from the pitchers. The hangover was still in control, but the cold water finally cleared my vision. "You twisted freak. Your revolution advocates beating women?" I was being sarcastic. I knew Milton didn't mean this, but I wanted to force him to win this argument rather than merely finish it. Partially because I knew that I was guilty too. I was hoping for redemption.

"Of course not. I detest all forms of violence, except perhaps violent upheaval against capitalist greed. My point is not to condone domestic violence, but merely to provide a rational explanation for the female reaction to it."

"It could be fear."

"Yes, but the metaphor would not support my argument, and in the end, it is the generation of an argument that supports my relationships and lifestyle that matters."

"The symmetry between domestic abuse and your relationships with women doesn't concern you?"

"Timothy, you must understand. I cannot create or undo anything about women. They are what they are. That they want their lovers to care about them is not of my doing. It only makes it possible for them to love me with all my imperfections."

I wasn't redeemed yet. "But then aren't you taking advantage of them? Or does an inherent weakness of their sex justify that?"

"I don't perceive this feminine tendency to be a weakness, and I'm not taking advantage of anyone. I do not own them. I am no capitalist."

I gave him a puzzled look as if to ask what capitalism had to do with women.

"The capitalist takes advantage of people by holding the means to their survival—money. Without money, the people cannot survive, so they must work for the capitalist, under the capitalist's conditions for employment. And if they don't, they starve to death, or their property is taken from them by a government that demands taxes, which is still servitude to the capitalist. The government functions as an extension of the capitalist's power. I, on the other hand, have no leverage over any man or woman. I provide only love, and she may take it from me or leave it and find comfort with any other man she chooses."

"Why not curtail your amorous bent and focus on one woman? Or does the revolution require that you act the libertine?"

Milton laughed, shrugged, and said, "Why?" Then he gave me a look that proclaimed in advance what he was about to say. Then he said it. "You don't." He must know about Holly.

I was convinced. To refute his claim, I would have to argue either that humans are by nature monogamous or that despite their natures they should be monogamous. I wasn't stupid enough to think that the first argument would fly. You can't justify morals on the basis of nature. And I didn't want to contemplate the second.

He had won. Thank God. But he also knew about Holly. Or at least, I thought he knew. Did he care? Why was he holding this back—to torture me with guilt so I would confess?

20

A GAGGING NOISE CAME from the back of the apartment, followed by the sound of a toilet flushing.

"The Arizona brothers are still a little ragged from last night." Milton signaled down the long, pale hall that led to the bedrooms and the bathroom. The gagging echoed off the walls. "It appears that at least one of the brothers will be unable to play this afternoon. You will have to take his place."

"Why is it I never know what you're talking about?"

"The Arizona brothers and I have a basketball game this afternoon. It is a very important game, as I have bet five hundred dollars that we can beat three members of the New Orleans adult league champions. I was rather counting on the brothers' teamwork, but we will manage without it if you can still rebound."

"I'm still confused. Why are you playing three New Orleans adult league champions for five hundred dollars? More importantly, why would you think I might be able to fill in for your, ah, brother?"

I wasn't comfortable distinguishing the brothers according to race, but I still didn't know their names and couldn't think of anything else to say that didn't sound silly.

"The Arizona brothers are brilliant basketball players. Didn't I mention that? Anyway, we regularly play three-on-three against other fellows, and we occasionally add a little financial incentive. We never lose."

"Never?" I asked. It seemed classic Milton hyperbole.

He shrugged. "Last Wednesday, I was at The Gin Mill on Magazine, and some guy there was bragging that the New Orleans adult league was so good that some of the better players could probably play pro. He included himself in that group. Naturally, I laughed at him and called him a witless drone. He was miffed by my incredulity. It seems that he was on the team that had lost in the finals, and he felt like the only possible explanation for this was that the other players were virtually professionals. I told him that if he was good enough to be a pro, he should have had little difficulty in dispatching any city league team and that I was certain he suffered from an overinflated opinion of his basketball skills and I could throw together a team of three, including myself, who could beat the best three guys he could find."

"Do you often talk like this to strangers?"

"Only to the morons, which means, yes, constantly. Anyway, to avoid the imminent fight, the bartender suggested that we play out the argument. We both agreed and bet five hundred dollars on the outcome. My adversary immediately got on the phone and tracked down one of the fellows from the five-man team that had beaten him in the final game. I believe the team we play today will be composed primarily of members of that team. While I suspect the Arizona brothers and I can beat them in any condition, I did bet five hundred cash and don't wish it to be a close thing."

I had hoped to play basketball while in town, but I was by no means a talented player and did not like the idea of playing in a game upon which such a large sum was riding. Especially not in my current condition— banged-up knee and acute hangover—and not against the league champions. Such a game was likely to turn unpleasant. But for the present, I was far more concerned with the evening's ball.

"I can't possibly play this afternoon."

"What?"

"I have a ball to attend this evening."

The black brother staggered into the room and collapsed onto the couch next to Milton.

"Please kill me," he moaned.

"I believe the aquavit rickey might be responsible for his condition," Milton said to me. He then dug between the couch cushions for a moment, produced a pocketknife, and tossed it to the black brother. He turned back to me: "It appears we will require your services this afternoon. The game is in less than an hour, so I don't imagine you will have time to go home and change. You'll have to borrow some clothes and a pair of shoes from us. I'm sure we can scrape up a pair that will fit."

"But—" I tried to interrupt but was unsuccessful.

"Don't 'but' me. You owe me. You would still be washing your face in that bathroom if I hadn't shown up and breathed some life into that party."

I could never argue with Milton. Even when I was right and knew he was wrong, he always seemed to get the better of me. I tried the soft approach. "My skills are not what they were, and as you know, they were never very good. Are you certain you want me to play?"

"Oh, it will be great fun. You can still dribble a bit, can't you?"

"I manage, but I can't play in your brother's shoes."

"He isn't my brother, and of course we'll find a pair of shoes to fit. Anyway, you said yourself you're not very good anymore. If that's true, then the shoes won't matter."

I was awed by his logic but pressed my point. "Don't you want to win?"

"God, man, of course we'll win! These guys are league champions. They have absolutely no chance of beating us. If there were going to be a referee present, we could probably beat the three of them with only two players. But as there will be no ref, I fear we will need the extra body for rebounding."

I was still confused. "But if they are league champs, aren't they good?"

"They are great, far better than we are. But that is why they'll lose so badly. Basketball is a game of statistics. The key statistic is shot percentage. If you defend close to the basket, the rest of the court is so open that the other team will invariably take many outside shots. They can't help themselves. Now, no matter how good they are, nobody hits from the outside all the time. But we'll only take layups. We can make almost one hundred percent of our layups, which means that so long as we pass the ball carefully—and the brothers and I are perfectly capable of doing that—then we'll score on every possession. Eventually, they'll miss an outside shot, and we'll win. It's simple math."

"But what if you miss a layup or they block your shots inside?"

"The statistics are still on our side. The brothers are downright capable players, and you know that I don't miss layups. They may block a few, and we will miss a few, but we won't miss more than they do. And that will be that. It never fails."

Milton was a big man, a very capable, physical man who could play basketball with shocking dexterity. He wasn't blowing smoke when he said that he wouldn't miss any layups against these players. If he got the ball within six feet of the basket, he would score.

"What about me?"

"Just play tough defense and only take layups that you can't miss. If you take a jump shot, then you must pay the five hundred dollars when we lose."

The white brother sauntered in half-naked, with a beer mug of water in one hand, a pair of black Chuck Taylors in the other, and a grotesque smile that betrayed unrelenting self-approval. "Shall we dance?"

"Scanda-fucking-navian blood," moaned the brother perishing on the couch.

To the smiling brother, Milton gave a knowing nod and said, "We must find Timothy a pair of shoes." Then to me, "What size do you wear?"

"Twelve or thirteen will do."

"Jesus! I had forgotten how big your feet are. You'll have to wear an old pair of mine. I have rather fat feet," Milton admitted, "and Chuck Taylors stretch out quite a bit. Still, I believe they will answer."

"What's with the Chuck Taylor motif? Will we all be wearing them?"

"Proletariat unity," said the white brother, sitting on the coffee table and fumbling with his shoes.

"Oh Christ. I've got to batter my feet on the basketball court for the sake of the revolution? Haven't you any real basketball shoes?" This entire experience was beginning to take on dreadful proportions.

"Chuck Taylors are real shoes."

"Only teenage punks wear them," I countered, hoping to make a point.

Milton stood up and turned the couch over backward, black brother and all. Beneath was a shoe graveyard. There must have been fifteen pairs, all worn-out, all Chuck Taylors.

"So that's the source of the curious perfume I detect?" I quipped.

Milton tossed me two shoes, dropped the couch heavily onto the hardwood floor, and shouted, "Saddle up! You'll find a pair of shorts, T-shirt, and socks somewhere in my room. I suggest you change before we leave."

"I'll need more ibuprofen and water if I'm going to pull this off," I announced, handing my empty pitcher to Milton. The black brother moaned.

21

THE BASKETBALL GAME went more or less according to plan. The other players were very good. Tall, fast, and aggressive. They were boasting about their city league victory and taunting us from the moment we arrived. Milton was very careful to ignore all of this and concerned himself only with the money, which he insisted be paid up front to a neutral third party. There was a little confusion on this point. His adversary from The Gin Mill apparently didn't bring enough, and Milton refused to play until the money was presented in full. The Gin Mill fellow suggested he was good for the difference and that we were not going to win anyway. He insisted that if we did win, he would get the rest of it to us. Milton found this unacceptable and told us to get back into the car, saying "We are going home." The league champions gave in and sent Mr. Gin Mill off to an ATM. Twenty minutes later, he returned with more cash. Milton counted the money slowly and deliberately, in clear view of everyone, suggesting that he doubted the counting skills of his opponents. This was obviously designed to rattle the other team, and it did. They got angry and threatened Milton with violence, but he only cursed them for interrupting him and started counting again, more slowly than before. I found the entire event very disturbing and would have left if I had driven. The likelihood of a fight seemed far greater than the likelihood of a basketball game. As unenthusiastic as I was about playing basketball with a raging hangover, I was even less enthusiastic about the prospects of being beaten up with a raging hangover.

In the end, it was a good thing Milton counted the money, because our opponents were ten dollars short. Milton pointed this out but then added ten dollars from his own wallet.

"Here, this is my gift to you. For ten dollars, we get the ball first. First team to fifty wins."

He then placed the money in a brown paper bag and handed it to the black brother, who was on the ground and propped up against the K-car so that he could watch. It was clear to everyone he wasn't going anywhere unless he was carried.

The other team was miffed and embarrassed, but they agreed to the terms since, according to the tallest one, "it wouldn't make any difference." Later, Milton confessed to me that he had secretly removed the bill from the bottom of the pile and pocketed it. Consequently, the ten-dollar bill he added to the bag was their own. He had done this both to unnerve them and to guarantee that we got the ball first.

Getting the ball first turned out to be the crucial play of the game, because we scored on the first possession. Milton then took the Arizona brother and me aside and reminded us that if we didn't miss any shots from here on, we would win, regardless of how well they shot the ball. Of course, that was no easy task, but Milton certainly held up his end of the bargain. He accurately predicted their overconfidence, which meant they played soft defense, thinking they would outscore us easily, and they began the game with a flurry of long jump shots, most of which they missed. As a rule, amateur players overestimate their ability to shoot from the outside, and these fellows were no exception.

I agreed to focus on defense, and I worked hard to box out and keep them off the glass. This meant that Milton cleaned up under the basket, easily rebounding all of their missed shots. He would then pass the ball to the Arizona brother, who would dribble down the court, wait until Milton got under the basket, and then pass it back to him. Milton was an easy target, especially with the other team playing such flaccid defense. You don't have to be big to play basketball, but it helps, and Milton put his massive frame to work, making his first ten shots. In short order, we enjoyed a handsome lead over the league players.

Sports analysts often discuss the importance of emotion, but basketball is a precision game and emotions are imprecise. While Milton played with a steady, unflappable demeanor, the league champions vacillated from gross overconfidence to palpable un-certainty. They attempted to recover their composure and play fundamental basketball, but this had never been their game plan, and they bickered among themselves regarding who should defend whom and who was at fault when Milton scored another easy layup. When The Gin Mill fellow who had initiated the contest with his boast missed a long, almost hopeless jump shot, our opponents fell into despair.

There was a good bit of shouting, cursing, and reminders that they were playing for five hundred dollars. In their despondency, they resorted to foul play—literally fouling Milton every time he attempted a shot. This was not unexpected, and Milton had prepared for it. Early in the game, Milton insisted that both teams were honorable, and therefore each player could call his own fouls. In their hopeless situation, the league players called fouls nearly every time they missed a defended shot. Milton accepted the fouls and allowed the other team to take the ball afresh on each occasion. With the additional chances, our opponents fared better, but not well enough to overcome our substantial opening lead. Milton never called a foul for himself, but none of the league players could stop his two hundred and fifty or so pounds driving to the hoop for easy layups. The league champs were tall, but they were lean, and their desperate and ineffective efforts to foul him only exacerbated their sense of helplessness. They pulled and pushed him, but he rarely missed a shot or failed to collect a rebound. We cruised to a comfortable victory, reaching the established fifty-point goal before the league champs reached forty.

Our victory was decisive, but The Gin Mill team insisted that we play a best two-out-of-three format. Milton would have none of it. At this point, things really got tense. It was not clear that these fellows were prepared to watch us walk off with five hundred of their dollars. The tallest league player bumped into the Arizona brother and then shoved him aggressively. He was easily a head taller than the brother and probably had fifty pounds on him.

"You want a piece of me?" the tall fellow asked.

Apparently, they thought that if they couldn't win the basketball game, perhaps they might win a fight after the game. The Arizona brother bristled. He was short and thin; muscular, yes, but clearly no match for this league champ brute. If my head had not hurt so badly, I would have panicked.

Milton answered the aggression in his typical, cavalier fashion. "If it is a fight you want, it is a fight you shall have. I will wager five hundred that this skinny white boy can kick your ass."

What had been an acute moment of tension suddenly felt very dangerous.

I did not approve of this turn of events and began to protest, but Milton silenced me with a glance. "Not only that, this skinny white boy from Arizona will take on any two of you for a thousand, all three of you for fifteen hundred."

For a moment, there was silence on the court. Everyone was on edge, except for Milton and the Arizona brother, both of whom affected an air of indifference. I suddenly realized they had done this before.

"Just come up with the money," Milton challenged him.

In an effort to end the uncomfortable silence, the big fellow suggested, "How 'bout I just kick his ass for nothing?" But the fight was out of him. Milton's challenge effectively reminded him that he had already been vanquished.

"Sorry, there is no such thing as a free lunch, or ass kicking, in this case," Milton said, shaking his head. "Even the simple pleasures come at a price. It is the burden of capitalism."

His economics lesson complete, Milton walked un obstructed to the black brother and said, "Let's go."

I limped to the car, my knee now the size of a grapefruit, and the four of us got into the K-car and drove away. Our defeated opponents could do nothing. They watched dejectedly as the K-car rumbled down the street. My knee really hurt.

22

MILTON STOPPED AT THE WINN-DIXIE on the way home and picked up a bottle of sherry, two bottles of Paisano, two bottles of bourbon, a case of beer, and four big bottles of some blue sports drink. We all went straight for the latter.

"Can you drop me off at my parents'?" I asked Milton. "I need to clean up, pick up my tuxedo, and get ready for tonight."

"Have you rented a tuxedo?"

"I don't own one."

"Indeed. From whom have you rented it?"

"I don't know. My mother made the arrangements. Someplace in Lakeside Mall."

"Well, we have to rent tuxedos for the Arizona brothers. We may as well all go together."

"Now?" I asked, wondering at the impression three sweat-drenched basketball players and a sick Arizona brother would make at the tuxedo shop.

"Yes, now. I would lend the brothers any of my own, but as you can see, neither of them possesses the physique to fill out my attire."

"I mean, shouldn't we clean up a bit first?"

"Yes, good thought." Milton turned off Magazine and onto Nashville Avenue. Moments later, we arrived at his apartment across the street from Ursuline Academy. We took turns with the shower. Fortunately, my suit with the torn slacks was at Milton's apartment. I shifted into these clothes, and when everyone was ready, we hopped back into the K-car. Milton had us at the tuxedo shop in fifteen minutes.

"That will do splendidly," Milton said to the store clerk, who was showing the Arizona brothers the only tuxedo style she had in stock that would fit them. It was a white affair with white tie and white cummerbund. They both frowned, as each was apparently hoping for something in black. "You'll look like knights in shining armor."

"We'll be shining all right," said the white brother.

"If they came with hoods, folks might think we were in the Ku Klux Klan," added the black brother.

"We'll look like idiots," continued the white brother.

The black brother pointed at me and the tuxedo my mother had ordered months ago. "How come he gets to wear black?"

"Because he has something you don't."

"What's that?"

"A mother who treats him like he is six years old. While it's normally a curse, it does guarantee him first pick of the tuxedos." Milton changed his tone. "Never fear, my brothers, at this event you will be nothing short of dashing, even if you were wearing pink tuxedos. I wore a white one to my prom, and although it did little to impress my date, it had a fine polyester finish and broad tie that repelled the numerous cocktails I poured down my front while drinking alone at the lake until dawn."

Milton's curious manner of changing the subject had again confused the issue. The brothers and I stared into space for a moment, imagining Milton as a rejected high schooler.

With us momentarily distracted, Milton turned to the sales girl and announced in his booming voice, "They will do splendidly."

And in a quieter voice, "Do you take credit?"

23

I CALLED MY MOTHER from Milton's apartment to assure her that I had picked up my tuxedo and would be in attendance that evening. She was quite beside herself with worry, not having seen me since brunch.

"Your brother has something particular planned for the ball but wouldn't tell me what it was. He said you knew."

I was silent.

"Do you know?" she asked, insisting on an answer.

"I have never had any notion of my brother's intentions. You should certainly know that by now, Mother."

"Will you be riding with us?"

"I wasn't planning on it. Do you need me?" I asked with all sincerity. Our family always seemed to have an endless supply of second cousins, and ugly cousins, who needed escorts. Why single women require escorts, when single men do not, I will never understand. It was never a difficult duty, for the cousins always ran off to join their friends as soon as they arrived. Apparently, single women only need an escort for their entrance. Once inside, they are free to roam about unescorted. I had once heard that my father escorted three different cousins into a ball, in addition to my mother, so that he had to leave and reenter repeatedly, each time with a different woman.

"We shall not need you unless Tabatha's date falls through or Sarah's husband fails to show up. You know how he hates these things."

"Who?" I asked.

"Walter, Sarah's husband."

"I don't blame him. I hate them too."

"Don't start."

"You can reach me at Milton's, if you need me," I sighed. "Ask Tabatha for the number."

"Tabatha?"

"Indeed. Until tonight, Mother." I hung up and leaned back into the old, familiar recliner in Milton's living room. I was alone for the moment, and it was the first time since I had arrived from Boston. I closed my eyes and basked in my solitude. Like the bent lounger I was stretched out in, I was completely out of sorts: confused, anxious, and desperate, and yet somehow it was a vital desperation. I felt alive; apprehensive but alive. In Boston, I was numb, lost. It was so easy to lose oneself in the great hustle and bustle there, and it had happened so quietly, as if it were nothing at all. Any other loss, an arm, a leg, a car, a wife, is certain to be noticed, but I had misplaced my sense of self without it even registering. I wanted to blame Boston for displacing me in its universal embracing of the possible, which, though magnificent and capable of grand strokes and gestures to humanity, risks losing sight of the individual. But as I sat in the peace and repose of Milton's recliner, this cultural criticism felt more and more like rationalizing. If, as Milton suggested, there really was no social mind and only social individuals, then there was no "Boston" to alienate me from myself. There were only other people, who on the whole had been fairly decent to me. There were only other people. And myself.

Milton walked in and disturbed my reflection. He was dressed in dashing black trousers, a voluminous white tuxedo shirt, and black wingtips. He was glowing, and I told him so. "You look radiant."

"I feel invincible," he said, standing before me with arms outstretched. "We were magnificent today."

"We were almost killed."

"In basketball?" he asked, surprised at my lack of faith.

"No, I mean in real life."

"Basketball is real life, and sometimes life requires some bumping and scraping in order to bring matters to a head, to force a resolution. There is nothing like the shattering of glass or the flow of blood to bring clarity of mind. Live life dangerously!"

"I could have done without the imminent threat of violence."

"But we could not have done it without you," Milton said with unguarded sincerity. "You were brilliant, just as I expected."

"I haven't played in years, and I was too hungover to see clearly," I answered, feeling embarrassed by his compliment. Milton could charm anyone.

"You scored the winning goal."

"The only shot I made." And that was only because the league players had moved to defend against Milton, who had been nearly unstoppable. He had received a pass from the Arizona brother, and all three defenders collapsed on him in an effort to prevent him from ending the game and with it their five hundred dollars. But before he was tackled, he had jumped, as if to make his patented layup, and instead executed a perfect behind-the-back pass to me, standing unguarded under the basket. It was my one attempt in the entire game, and while I am no basketball wizard, even I couldn't miss such a simple layup.

"It was the winning shot," he reminded me, "and as such, it was the most important." He walked to a tall, wooden cabinet beside the TVs and retrieved a bottle of sherry and two glasses from inside. "Do you care for a glass? I find it refreshing after a vigorous enterprise."

"Please."

Milton poured us both a short glass and set the glasses and the bottle on the coffee table in front of me.

"We have some time while the Arizona brothers struggle with their costumes. I don't know if they have ever worn tuxedos before, at least not when they were sober."

Milton disappeared into the kitchen and returned with two pill bottles. He emptied the contents of both onto the coffee table and said, "Ibuprofen or aspirin, choose your poison." The tablets were now mixed, and as I reached for them I recalled some hazard about taking them together: Was it erectile dysfunction, irritable bowel, blindness? I paused a moment, shrugged, grabbed four pills of brownish hue, and took them with a large swallow of sherry. It was an excellent sherry and, as Milton predicted, astonishingly refreshing after our exertions.

"As we have a moment, let us talk about your evening. What are we going to do about William and Jane?"

"We?" I asked.

"Yes, we. I know that you have been waiting for me to derive a solution to this problem of yours. Well, I have got it, and it is as simple as 'kiss my hand.'"

I finished my sherry and handed him the empty glass.

"Kiss my hand? What do you have in mind?"

"Well, as I see it, we have two options." Milton refilled my glass and returned it to me. "The first is simple and straightforward but requires a very steady hand and cunning mind. So we must opt for the second."

"Thank you."

"Sorry, my dear, but on occasions like these, we must not succumb to illusions of grandeur. You have never been exceedingly cool under pressure, and there is no reason to believe that you developed such talents in Boston."

I sighed and started in on the second glass of sherry.

"Option two: The brothers and I mug William and toss him into the trunk of the K-car. You toss Jane into your parents' car and make a run for it. If you succeed, you live happily ever after. If you fail, you return to the party and pursue debutantes like the rest of us."

"Succeed?" I was confused. "At what? Tossing her into the car?"

"Idiot," Milton shook his head and took a healthy gulp of sherry as if bracing himself for a confrontation. "You must seduce her."

"Why? So your debutante victims won't be distracted by the announcement of an engagement?"

Milton averred, "First, maintaining the integrity of the hunting ground certainly justifies a simple seduction and, perhaps, even throwing your brother into the trunk of our car."

I shook my head disapprovingly, but he continued.

"More importantly, no seduction of a beautiful woman should require any justification, especially not when it is the woman you love."

"Love?"

"Love."

I was not comfortable with the use of the word love, but I wasn't prepared to argue about Jane. I changed the subject. "And William?"

"We dump him in City Park. The walk home will cool him off."

"That sounds prefect, so long as you kill William," I suggested and knocked back the rest of my sherry. "He works for the DA and will not hesitate to have us all thrown in prison."

"OK, Mr. Smarty. Do you have a better idea?"

"I don't know what to do. I never know," I admitted. My track record wasn't good, and the last twenty-four hours had demonstrated no improvement on my part. It was the only thing about which I was certain: that I was uncertain about everything.

"That, my dear, is your problem. You must simply choose. And as a faithful servant of Søren Kierkegaard, I recommend that you choose the most absurd path possible."

"You mean, work to bring about the revolution like you?"

"Well, yes, if you were up to it. But I fear you haven't the mind for revolutionary detail. No, the solution to the Jane dilemma must be something that runs contrary to your nature."

"Nature? Since when did human nature come into existential calculation?" I asked, believing I had caught Milton off his philosophical guard. I could distinctly recall Jean-Paul Sartre's essay on existentialism in which he denied the existence of any pre-given human nature.

"You are thinking of French existentialism, if I follow you correctly. Never take seriously anything a Frenchman tells you, unless it has to do with making love or invading Austria."

"Didn't you say this was a matter of love?" I asked.

"Do not presume to get analytical with me," Milton replied. "I said it was a problem. That the problem is to do with love does not mean that the problem is love."

He put his glass of sherry to his lips, paused, and then said, "No, no, the problem requires that you do something dramatic."

"Meaning that it's my nature to avoid drama?"

"Meaning that it is has been your nature to avoid doing something that you might regret. This is why you have always ignored my good advice. You wonder, 'Will I regret confessing my love? Will I regret having done nothing?' It doesn't matter what you choose. You will regret both."

"You mean regarding Jane?" I asked.

"Yes, but perhaps not limited to Jane."

"Lovely."

Milton paused to savor his sherry. "So back to your problem. Here's how it will work. The brothers and I will collect a passel of nubile lasses and use them to distract your brother. This should keep him busy for quite some time. If not, we toss him into the trunk. Meanwhile, you make your move with Jane."

"Yes, that seems very clever. But exactly what do you propose I say to her?"

"Certainly not what you said last night. I might try something more romantic."

"Oh yes, something like this: 'Hi, Jane. While I have arranged to have my brother abducted, I thought I would take this opportunity to read you some poetry.'"

"That would be better than whatever it was you said last night. If you get stuck, ask Roberto."

"The Italian?"

"Yes."

"He's going to be there? This is supposed to be a private party, and yet it appears that everyone you know will be there."

"I told you, I am always invited to the best parties, and I make certain that my friends are included. Anyway, Roberto did a favor for your mother once, escorting a homely niece of hers. I arranged it. She has been eternally grateful."

24

I T WAS SIX BEFORE the Arizona brothers emerged
from their bedroom, handsomely clad in white. They
were pleased to see that Roberto had arrived with three
tremendous dishes of antipasto: fine meats, olives,
cheeses, marinated vegetables, and four loaves of French
bread. There was enough food to feed twenty, but the
way we set to it, it was clear it would not survive the five
of us. We all took places around the worn wooden table
in the dining room. Milton brought out two bottles of
Paisano, a pitcher of water, a fresh supply of pain pills,
and myriad glasses, small plates, and forks. My body
craved food. Skipping out on brunch early and playing
basketball on nothing but a hangover and two bowls of
ice cream had left me prepared to eat my hand. I spoke
only to ask for more wine or water, alternating between
the two to cleanse my palate between dishes.

After an initial silence during which everyone gorged
himself, we all assumed a more casual pace and began
discussing the day's events: the brunch, the basketball
game, and the upcoming ball. The brothers spoke of
women, how to find them, how to seduce them. Both

professed a great body of knowledge on the subject. Then Roberto spoke of love.

"People who talk about love make love," he reminded us repeatedly in his heavy Italian accent. Everyone stopped speaking to listen. Clearly, Roberto was the recognized master of the subject at this table. "When you meet the girl, do not bother her with any other subject. Do not speak of the work or the school or the hobbies." Roberto paused to shove three enormous olives into his mouth. Through a mouthful he explained, "Women have no interests apart from love. Everything else they do is, is, is—I don't know how you say—"

"Pretense?" inserted Milton.

"Hmmm. I don't know this 'pretense' but perhaps. I will say it is nothing. Women only make the hobbies, the work, the school to find a man, to make love. So if you speak of these other things, you are wasting her time."

"Amen," agreed the black brother.

Roberto continued. "Tell her she is beautiful. Tell her you love her. Tell her you want to make the love to her."

"Hear him," said the white brother.

"Be cautious of the talkative girl," warned Milton. "The one who approaches you with a phalanx of questions and shows infinite interest in you. She is faking it. She has been coached by her mother and will absorb your entire evening in useless prattle before being whisked away by a relative who has been secretly observing the entire charade. She will be gone, and you will go home empty-handed."

"Are you bringing your girlfriends?" I asked Milton, hoping to derail his bravado.

"I am sure I don't know what you are talking about," Milton answered with a perfectly straight face.

"We can't all fit in the K-car if you are dragging your entourage along," added the black brother, joining my critique of Milton.

"Well, isn't this a fine situation I find myself in? My propriety attacked in my own home," Milton feigned injury. Roberto offered a toast to Milton's propriety, and everyone drank. After refilling his glass and passing the wine on, Milton added, "For your information, I am going stag tonight."

Chuckles from the brothers.

Milton continued. "Things may be more complicated than I expected. The debutante party Holly is attending turns out to be the same one we are attending, so at least two of my female acquaintances will be present."

Chuckles from everyone, save me.

"It's only a minor setback."

"Are they your dates?" I asked, while trying desperately to erase a rather persistent image of my sister on one of Milton's curious double engagements. "I trust you won't need my help again. Maybe I should see to your sick aunt?"

"Of course not," Milton shot back. "These girls are not my dates. Think of them rather as, ah, cologne, if you will."

"Cologne?" I asked, struggling to make sense of this image.

"Precisely. They make the hunting so much easier."

Roberto nodded agreement, but the rest of us looked confused.

"You're confused," Milton said, noticing the looks on our faces. "Allow me to explain. A group of single men casting about for unescorted women smells like week-old oysters. A man surrounded by women is clearly a catch. Far better to move from one girl to the next, allowing the girls to make the introductions. The air of formality dampens the building of amour and allows you to take the girls off guard. Women want romance, of course, but they are generally afraid of it. The naked truth of sexuality horrifies and humiliates them. They prefer to be taken by surprise, swept up and away."

"That is why it is so difficult to pick up women in a bar," announced the white brother in something akin to an epiphany.

"Because they expect it?" I asked.

"Precisely."

I had to wonder if my sister was the old girl or the new girl. "You should write a book," I quipped and tossed back a generous slice of Parmesan cheese.

Milton ignored me. "Women love romance, but romance must be unexpected, full of mystery and suspense. The well-foreseen, frontal assault rarely works, except in Metairie where the girls are blunted by large quantities of frozen daiquiris. But we will not be in Metairie tonight, gentlemen. It's nothing but young ladies and women of society."

"But women are women. They want love," added Roberto between a slice of prosciutto and a piece of French bread dipped in olive oil.

"Indeed. Deep down inside, they are all the same. The only difference at a debutante ball in New Orleans

is that you must take them by cunning, not by storm."
Milton's soliloquy delighted the ears as much as the
antipasto delighted the tongue. "Never let them know
they are being seduced. Let them dream of being
seduced, and they will seduce themselves. Remember,
if the conversation begins to take an ugly turn, always
redirect it in conjunction with a compliment, preferably
of a biological nature. It sounds silly, but it never fails."

"Is this what you did to my little sister?" I couldn't
hold back.

"Your sister is the epitome of charm and decency,"
Milton lied. I knew he was lying. He knew I knew he
was lying. He was being polite. There is never any safe
way to successfully rebuff polite. You always come out
the loser. So I let the lie lie. "It is my honor that she
shows me the slightest interest."

The phone rang. Milton ignored it, allowing the
machine to pick it up.

"Handy's Massage Parlor," the machine answered.

Milton shrugged. "I change the messages daily. Keeps
the creditors at bay."

My mother's voice emerged through the speaker.

"Jesus Christ, I thought this was the number—
Tabatha! Tabatha! Didn't you say this was the right
number?"

I leaped to my feet and picked up the receiver, ending
an ugly glimpse into my home life.

"Yes, Mother?"

"Jesus, Timothy, is that you?"

"Yes, Mother."

"At a massage parlor?"

"No, Mother, it's just Milton's machine."

"Christ, I wish he would change it. It's indecent."

"I think that's the point."

"Anyway, we will need you this evening."

"What?" I was just starting to enjoy the feel of graduate student life again, sitting around a table drinking, eating, and talking endlessly about love, politics, and the art of living, drifting from one subject to the next, unencumbered by deadlines, utility, and profits. Roberto had said that people who talk of love make love, but he had failed to recognize the universal in his claim. People who talk of the world make the world. That's how the philosophers made our world, by speaking it into existence. No one epitomizes the love of discourse more than grad students. To the casual observer, the graduate student may seem a lusty ne'er-do-well, but graduate students of the world may be the thin, drunk line between civilization and barbarism. Without them, chaos. My mother's demands threatened our very civilization.

"Your sister's date has canceled," my mother announced.

"Oh God."

"For the life of me, I don't understand this generation. Something about a ruptured appendix. I can't imagine it couldn't wait until tomorrow. No sense of responsibility." My mother was taking on an all-too-familiar tone.

"Why can't James escort her? He seemed to handle brunch perfectly," meaning he had never said a word and avoided spilling anything.

"He is escorting her, but he was supposed to escort your sister Sarah. So now you will have to escort Sarah."

They were really working poor James to the bone.

"What about Sarah's husband?"

"Don't get me started on him. He's useless."

"What about her agoraphobia?"

"Timothy!"

"OK."

"Please come at once. We are leaving shortly."

"I haven't a car. Can you pick me up?"

"It's not enough I have your sisters to look after, now you come home and I must look after you too," she muttered and added something I didn't understand. "I will send your aunt. Where are you?"

I returned to the table after giving driving instructions to my mother. The conversation had wandered from women to Milton's revolution, or had it? It was surprising how similar the two were.

The black brother was standing, arms spread, wineglass in hand. "I would never profess some trite aphorism as a remedy for an existential crisis."

His white brother put a hand on his shoulder, signaling him to sit. "We are all victims of our material conditions," the white brother sighed.

Milton tossed back a handful of olives, chased them with the Paisano, and addressed the table as he was wont to do. "The higher we rise, the more integrated we become in the workings of history, the less freedom we enjoy." Everyone nodded in agreement. "The great heroes of nations play their little parts, pursue their pathetic self-interest, achieve political or personal fame, unaware that they are pawns in the total plan of destiny. But are they ever really happy, collecting their trinkets and certificates of participation in the hamster wheel of capitalism? Their whole life is labor and trouble, and when their part is played, they are cast off like empty hulls from the kernel. They die young like Alexander, are murdered like Caesar, are imprisoned like Napoleon, are mocked like Ayn Rand."

The black brother raised his glass, "To mocking Ayn Rand."

"To mocking Ayn Rand," everyone said.

The white brother completed both the toast and Milton's Hegelian rant with Shakespearean flair: "No my friends, we attain liberty by dodging the slings and arrows of outrageous fortune, by avoiding responsibility, significance, and purpose."

The Arizona brothers played the ne'er-do-well part to perfection, but at least they knew they were alive, which was more than I could say for myself these past three years. I had done everything a man is expected to do: find a job, find an apartment, find a girl to marry.

I was in an existential crisis. And Milton could tell. He seized my forlorn look as cue to continue in his oration, briefly explaining that such a crisis could serve as a reminder of the need to disentangle ourselves from the day-to-day workings of history in order to maintain an authentic perspective on it. "The necessary revolutionary insight and zeal," he professed, "could not manifest in a soul burdened with everyday life."

"Disengaged intellectuals must lead the revolution of the disaffected?" I asked.

"Exactly," Milton said. "Marx was wrong in only one regard. He felt that the communists must oppose capitalism directly. But this open rebellion was destined to fail in the industrialized nations—precisely those nations capable of producing enough bread and circuses to quell any popular movement. A full belly is the enemy of revolution."

Milton took a dramatic pause to develop the suspense.

"The industrialized nations require a stealth revolution, a revolution that exploits the capitalists' insatiable greed, shocking lack of creativity, and unwarranted self-confidence. A revolution that preys upon the ethic of the free market: that you can buy happiness. If that premise were true, then the more you buy, the happier you should be. Modern capitalism has survived this long only because of the monastic ethic of the Middle Ages. The prudence and self-control of the Middle Ages have kept the full force of our capitalist greed in check."

Everyone nodded. Milton stood up and raised his glass. "It is our job, gentlemen, to release this greed and show the world what it has truly become. Once released, the capitalist ethic will consume itself. In an absurd quest for happiness, the people will spend every penny. They will buy insatiably, for fear that they may die before they find true happiness. The debt will soar, and the debtors will ultimately default, leaving the economy in ruin."

Clearly, Milton had given this lecture before, probably to his freshman philosophy class. What a lovely irony that the students' capitalist parents were paying thirty-five grand a year in tuition to have their children educated by their sworn enemy: the hard-drinking, womanizing, leader of the new communist revolution.

For his prognosis, Milton received a round of cheers. "In the ashes of this sinful empire, a new world order will arise. A communism of people, wherein all shall be equal and all shall share the burden of work"—there was some grumbling from the brothers—"and leisure," he added, and everyone cheered again. I, too, cheered with gusto.

"Hurrah for the revolution!"

"To the revolution!"

"May we be cleansed of materialism, but not yet."

"The revolution will make great strides tonight," Milton emphasized. "We begin with the seduction of the capitalists' women."

A horn sounded outside. My Aunt Dee, I assumed. I quickly finished a handful of olives, two handsome slices of smelly cheese, a piece of bread, and a glass of Paisano. With my mouth full, I stood and addressed Milton's band of rogues.

"I will see you at the ball. Good hunting."

I turned, grabbed my tuxedo jacket from the back of my chair, and hurried to the door, though not before my aunt had sounded her horn a second time.

"Good hunting" and "See you there" echoed from the table as I made my exit.

THE PARTY

Remember, remember always that all of
us, and you and I especially, are descended
from immigrants and revolutionists.

Franklin D. Roosevelt

GIN & TONIC

2 OZ GIN
4 OZ TONIC
1 LIME WEDGE

Serve in a rocks glass over ice.

25

AFTER WHAT SEEMED AN ETERNITY of primping, poking, shouting, and a few tears, Tabatha was finally made ready for the party. It was technically a party, not a ball we were attending that evening. The balls coincide with Mardi Gras celebrations, while a series of coming out parties in the summer or around Christmas precede these balls. The distinction seemed unimportant to me but clearly stood out in the financial side of my father's brain. He was grumbling about the cost of the party dresses, the cost of ball dresses, and the great savings he might realize if ever someone could contrive to develop a dress that would cover the not dissimilar demands of a party and a ball. Like me, he had never fully appreciated the nuances of the debutante ritual. We sat together in the living room, drinking brandy and watching a television documentary about hyenas and lions. My father made certain that my glass did not stay empty.

"You cannot approach these events on an empty stomach," he warned. "Drink up."

Other than this, he only groused under his breath about the party. He seemed to be steeling himself for a great battle.

The women descended the stairs in chronological order, from top to bottom. My aunts, my mother, Sarah, and then Tabatha, each introducing the next as they came and each shouting instructions at Tabatha not to forget something: purse, makeup, leave the purse, brush, leave the brush, earrings. They were in evening gowns of different colors and dimensions. The older women wore long, sequined dresses, with the number of sequins in seeming proportion to the woman's age.

Sarah wore a royal blue, velvet garment with a plunging neckline that came to rest casually along the rise of her bosom, a bosom that benefited from the latest in bra technology. Her hair was done up, with a single ivory comb to hold it in place.

Tabatha appeared in a simple, sleek silk dress the color of cognac. She wore no rings or earrings, only a modest pearl necklace my father had bought for her sixteenth birthday. Her lips and fingernails were painted to accent her dress. She was aglow, with a delicate beauty and youthful potency. I had always known my sisters were quite fetching, but this evening they truly outdid themselves.

My father ignored them all until the last had reached the landing. He finished his drink, scrambled to his feet, and released a volley of well-rehearsed compliments upon the whole troupe: beautiful, stunning, charming, absolutely, yes, yes. He tipped his glass to them and tried to drain it again, but discovered he had already done so and offered himself a refill for the road.

The patriarchal praise completed, my mother returned to giving orders. There was some discussion of transport, who would ride with whom, but most of that appeared to have been settled already. Sarah and I were both sent upstairs to recover more items: purse, keys, brush, lipstick, not that lipstick, the lipstick on the dresser, never mind the purse, it's down here, the keys are in it.

"How are you, Sarah?" I asked. I hadn't really spoken to her since I had been home, except when she accosted me at the door earlier that morning.

"Well enough, I suppose. Nice escape you pulled off at brunch today. Did you have to pay Milton to get you out of there?" she asked in a serpent-like strike designed to inspire guilt. Guilt was an emotion she encouraged in others. She would have made an excellent nun or missionary.

"You spent far too many years in Catholic school," I told her, "and, no, he provided me the service free of charge, unless you believe your sister to have some value."

"Tabatha? No," she said plainly. "You've been around Milton too long. You are beginning to sound like him. It's obnoxious." She paused and turned her head to a slight angle. She was thinking. I chose not to interrupt this rare moment. "You mean that Milton is interested in Tabatha?"

"I believe that it may be mutual, but I can't be sure."

As we were discussing relationships, I decided to inquire into hers. "How's your husband?"

"Fine, I guess," she said as if very tired of that subject.

"He isn't coming tonight?"

She just glared at me.

"Sorry."

"He doesn't believe I am sick," she asserted over shouts from my mother to hurry up.

"Sick?" I asked and then wished I hadn't.

"Yes. It's dreadful, and nobody takes it seriously."

"Yes, of course." I was trying to disengage gracefully.

"Sometimes I think he is the one who makes me sick."

Must stop her. Must stop her. She will go on all night in this dreary tone and utterly destroy the evening. It was bad enough to be stuck with a whining woman all night, but a whining sister? Then it hit me: Milton's recommendation that you can save any conversation with a well-placed compliment.

"It will be a delight to escort you, Sarah. I have not had a chance to speak with you in ages. You look ravishing."

It was an absurd change, of course, but the compliment at the end carried the day, just as Milton predicted. Sarah smiled and retrieved a lipstick on the dresser. I felt a surge of energy flowing through my very tired bones. Perhaps tonight was my night. Perhaps I could pull it off. Pull what off? The question remained: Did I wish to pull off anything? My mother shouted, and we headed downstairs and joined the others waiting at the cars.

The loading and unloading of partygoers went smoothly, and we arrived at the New Orleans Country Club just after dark. I had always liked the country club, a splendid old structure that hearkened back to a kinder, gentler South that never really existed. With its sweeping stairwell leading to a gracious entrance, framed against a mustard brick façade, it looked like it belonged uptown on St. Charles Avenue. In a rather unfortunate twist of geography, however, one found the exclusive establishment set back only slightly from the I-10 viaduct just outside the city, tucked tightly between the cemetery and Jefferson Parish. Bordered by cultural death on one side and actual dead people on the other, it failed to conjure the image of old Southern aristocracy, and the eighteen-wheel tractor-trailers rushing along the overpass dispelled any trace of the nineteenth-century glory the architects were hoping to revive. Nonetheless, surrounded by grand oaks, it was pleasant enough, certainly pleasant enough for a debutante party. More important than the atmosphere, the location put the club well outside the calming boundaries of uptown and underscored the horrors awaiting me inside. I would be forced to endure Jane and William's announcement, avoid Holly's father, watch Milton seduce my sister, and keep Roberto and the Arizona brothers out of trouble.

I entered the central ballroom through the main foyer with Sarah by my side. She had taken my arm at the car and released it the moment we crossed the threshold. I wondered if her antipathy toward human contact was specific to me or more universal and if this antipathy might explain the strain in her marriage. As her arm slipped away, I resolved to risk offending her and ask, but the decision came too late. Sarah turned from me and joined Tabatha, who was whisked away to have the jostle of the drive primped out of her by my mother and aunts. They made their way to the women's powder room, and with my escort obligation satisfied, I stood alone feeling unpleasantly purposeless. Noticing the frail figure I cut, my father walked over, put an encouraging hand on my shoulder, and suggested that we find the bar.

The place was already sprinkled with folks busying themselves with gossip and worry. The Trenchards were there, with additional members of the family, dates, and assorted hangers-on. I was relieved not to see Holly or her family. I imagined she must also be in the dressing room being poked and prodded, a process that sometimes required the entire entourage. Working around the early arrivals, the staff was frantically setting tables, stocking the bar, and putting the finishing touches on a low stage for the band in the grand ballroom. This main ballroom would shelter the receiving line at the beginning of the party, provide a sumptuous table of hors d'oeuvres, and ultimately serve as the dance hall toward the end. There were three ballrooms adjacent to it—one on each side and one behind. This evening, only the main ballroom and the room to the right were being used.

My father and I resumed our nearly silent companionship, and we slipped past a host of employees working like ants to decorate the base of a magnificent ice sculpture of a swan, with wings spread, that sat guard over the hors d'oeuvres. We paused briefly before the chilly monstrosity, and my father commented on the cost. "Your mother insisted on a swan."

"It's very elegant," I said.

"A century ago, a father was expected to provide his daughter with a dowry. Now, it seems, fathers are expected to provide swans," he sighed. "It is a new world out there, son. I suppose these affairs have always been something of a charade. Still, it afforded a girl the opportunity to put her best foot forward with the finest families in town, and that was worth something. Now, well, I can't tell what the whole thing is about anymore."

"It's a lovely party," I said, hoping to console him.

"It's your inheritance, so we might as well enjoy it. Let's have a drink."

We continued our walk to the long bar set up at the far end of the smaller ballroom. When it wasn't the debutante season, the room operated as a dining hall, but this evening it served as an extension of the main ballroom, with the two connected by a doorway large enough to allow a car to pass without fear. The bar was unoccupied except for the bartender, who was busy stocking the shelves at the expense of my birthright. My father selected stools that offered a commanding view of both rooms, so that we could observe the party unfolding at a safe distance. He offered the attendant ten dollars and asked him to pour us each a tall gin and tonic. Even though it was an open bar, my father always insisted on tipping heavily to "ensure you get a well-made drink." I wasn't sure that my constitution could handle any more well-made drinks. My twenty-four-hour drinking, dancing, and basketball binge left me feeling wraithlike. The antipasto had provided temporary relief, but its medicinal effects were wearing off—or else I was drinking them off. I could feel my legs stiffening and my head spinning. The bartender produced two gin and tonics in tall glasses topped with lime wedges, and

I wondered if I could get through this whole thing and remain conscious.

"If I drink all of this, I may pass out," I warned my father.

"Then I would drink it quickly, if I were you."

As we spoke, a second host of servers brought forth trays of oysters Bienville, oysters Rockefeller, oysters Suzette, oysters en brochette, raw oysters, smoked oysters, stuffed crabs, stuffed shrimp, boiled shrimp, baked shrimp, stuffed artichoke hearts, crawfish Amandine, along with shrimp and crawfish étouffées in large chafing dishes. My father's tipping practice proved its worth, as the bartender signaled a coworker who promptly delivered two large platters of oysters for our nourishment.

26

I DON'T KNOW HOW LONG we sat drinking gin and eating oysters. Ten-dollar bills produced more of the twelve-ounce gin and tonics and additional trays of shrimp and crawfish. I had just forgotten how much I disliked debutante balls when I felt a tug at my sleeve. It was Sarah.

"Timothy, Father, you must join the receiving line."

I turned from my drink to see that the ballroom was filling up. The carefully dressed debutantes and their parents had formed a line at the door and were welcoming New Orleans' finest. There was Tabatha, Holly, and Elizabeth, each radiating enough charm to light the city. Even Elizabeth's complexion seemed improved in the festive atmosphere. I didn't fancy the idea of standing in line with Holly and her parents, as I was certain her father would finger me for this morning's burglary.

I sent Sarah away with assurances that we would join them immediately after I visited the restroom. She hissed at me disapprovingly and walked back toward the line. My father had used the restroom as a means of escape for years, and Sarah must have sensed I was borrowing his move. But it wasn't the restroom or the receiving line that concerned me. It was Jane. I needed to speak with her before William made his announcement. I wasn't sure what I would say, but I had to say something. I finished my drink, excused myself from the bar, and began to traverse the hall. I walked slowly, inspecting the crowded room, looking for Jane or William. The sea of round tables decorated with grand flower arrangements provided excellent cover for the guests. It would be easy to get lost in the throng.

I stopped in the middle of the room and did a careful full-circle turn. No Jane. No William. I bumped into a tuxedo-clad gentleman of about sixty years. The collision caused him to drop his drink, which fell to the ground, bounced twice, and finally rolled under the dress of a tall, handsome woman. She was unaware of the glass. With well-mannered panache, the gentleman apologized to me for his clumsiness and insisted that he be allowed to buy me a drink. He instantly put his arm around me before I could respond and steered me back to the bar where my father still loitered. Many would have been fooled by his courtesy, but I could tell he was using me as a diversion from some dreaded duty or dreaded someone—probably his wife. We arrived at the bar and he introduced me to my father, who put out his hand. The gentleman, who never bothered to introduce himself, ordered us all gin and tonics and dropped a dollar tip on the bar. My father just held out his half-full glass. The bartender generously replenished it and then whipped up two fresh drinks.

"Lovely young lady," said the gentleman, motioning over my shoulder.

I turned to see Holly approaching. I looked for an escape route, but I was cornered.

"Well, well, lad, looks like you're in luck," he added, as it became clear she was coming to speak with me.

I finished my drink quickly, which helped to repress the fight-or-flight instinct.

"No place to run here," my father added, recognizing my distress. Both men laughed and returned to their drinks and a conversation that sounded as if it had been going for hours, maybe years.

"Are you the famous cat thief I've read about in the papers?" Holly asked.

I couldn't help but smile. She really was quite lovely. She wore a dazzling silver ball gown that ducked and dipped tightly about the curves of her body, landing gracefully an inch above the floor, giving the impression that she was levitating rather than walking. Her golden-blonde hair cascaded across nearly bare shoulders like a waterfall of magnolia petals. Milton could really pick them. I pointed to the service doors at the back of the ballroom. She took my arm as if to be led, but she did the leading. I could hear the unnamed gentleman muttering something to my father about youth being wasted on the young or maybe simply just youth being wasted. I turned back to look, as if making eye contact would clarify the comment, but they were now surrounded by women their own age, and both men turned sullen and dejected.

Holly and I passed through the doors into the kitchen and were politely ignored by the busy country club staff preparing more plates of oysters, shrimp, and crawfish. We found our way to the rear exit of the building. Since Holly had initiated the walk, I decided to allow her to initiate the conversation. But she seemed content in the silence. We strolled toward what appeared to be an extensive garden, though in the light of day I knew it was the club's golf course.

"Do you golf?" she asked flatly.

"The tie?" I figured she remembered it.

"Of course the tie—and your family. Your family looks like the golfing type."

"No, never had much appeal to me. My brother and father play."

"Basketball then? I know that's all Milton talks about."

"Yeah. I prefer basketball, but I don't play particularly well. Not like Milton. Did you hear about our victory this afternoon?" I asked with a little pride.

"No. I only knew he and the brothers were planning to play. I didn't know you intended to join them."

"I wasn't supposed to, but one of the brothers was a bit out of sorts come game time."

She nodded knowingly. "What about your knee?"

"It hurt, but I survived."

"And Milton?"

"Milton was brilliant," I continued, "single-handedly won the game, hangover and all. I don't know how he does it."

"Yeah, well, I don't either. And, well," she paused, looked down, shuffled her shiny silver pumps, and then fixed me with eyes that flashed like sapphires reflecting the light of the stars. Or perhaps it was the headlights of the cars still arriving in valet parking. "I didn't bring you out here to talk about basketball."

She paused again, but I decided to exercise caution. I waited.

She continued in a nervous but determined tone. "I wanted to talk about us."

Roberto had been right again. It's always about love. I gave a short, unintentional laugh that I quickly transformed into a cough for the sake of the moment. I began to speak but decided that anything I said would be dangerous. If I sounded uninterested, she would be hurt, even if she was uninterested. No woman wants a man to express disinterest after a night of whatever it was we did, even if she's not interested herself. But at the same time, I didn't want to say something that would encourage her affection, because the last thing I needed was to add another degree of difficulty to the evening. I was desperate to avoid a scene, but Holly's grace, beauty, and charm were confounding my judgment. Remain silent, remain silent, remain silent, I said to myself. Wait for her to speak first.

I said nothing.

We continued to walk, arm in arm, like lovers. The pressure was building, something had to be said or done soon. She waited with a hunter's patience, seeming content to stroll like this, just the two of us, for the entire evening. The headlights from the cars cast shafts of light through the foliage of the great trees, such that I felt like we were surrounded by ever-dancing shadows and ghosts, ghosts witnessing my social discomfiture. Why was there always an audience when I was likely to humiliate myself? Holly steered us away from the parking lot into the open of a fairway. The stars were blotted out by the orange haze of the city, cloaking the golf course in an apocalyptic light. Not exactly romantic, but out there, under an orange sky, accompanied only by halogen spirits dancing in the trees, I felt as if we were the last man and woman in the wake of Armageddon, and I enjoyed it, the artificial nature of the golf course and the genuine warmth of being with Holly.

What would she say? I began to weaken and consider conversation options. Every thought that came to mind was sophomoric. Remain silent, remain silent, remain silent. I was resolved. I remained silent. I said nothing.

We arrived at a green and stopped. The grass was short and tight, like walking on a three-day-old beard. Remain silent—but something was trying to come out. I suppressed it. I walked over and tweaked the flag so that it flopped back and forth on its fiberglass pole, waving a surrender. Holly just watched me, as if sizing me up. I felt as though I had failed to meet her standards, whatever they were. I looked at the flag, then at Holly, then back at the flag that had stopped flapping and hung motionless from the pole. I tried to think of something clever to say, about the flag, the pole, the golf course, the orange sky, but nothing clever emerged. Nonetheless words wanted to come out. I couldn't stop them. I was going to say something, even if I didn't want to say anything. But the words were rising up from the depths. At least say something intelligent, I told myself.

I spoke.

I said, "Err."

It didn't come out as I had hoped, but there it was, a sound thrown into the void. I started with this burble hoping that the proper words would follow, but they didn't. So there it was. My best effort at a discourse on love. If people who speak about love make love, I was facing a lifetime of celibacy. She turned and looked at me. I had to say something else now, but what?

"Are your parents still pursuing the burglar?" I was sincerely worried that her father would have me arrested, but it was not worthy of the moment. At least it was a complete sentence.

She laughed. "Yes. My father is out of his mind. He's called the police, the mayor's office. He even dragged my brother down to the police station to look at photos of known criminals. I thought they only did that in movies. Anyway, you're in the clear. My brother isn't here tonight, some Boy Scout thing, and my father was wearing his reading glasses when he saw you. You were only a blur. He could never identify you."

"His reading glasses?" It sounded unlikely.

"Yeah, he was reading the paper and drinking coffee when you attempted your breakout. He has terrible vision. He uses one pair of glasses to read and another for everyday stuff. In his rush to the front door, he failed to grab his other pair, which means he saw you through reading glasses. Don't linger around him and you should be fine."

"That's quite a relief. I was afraid the police would arrive any minute."

She paused and looked at me intently. "But what about us?"

She wasn't going to let it go. I had to say something. You can ignore a question once, but twice?

"I don't know? How do you feel?"

It wasn't brilliant, but it was an improvement over "err."

"Like a slut."

"Pardon?" I was expecting an outpouring of emotion. Not a concern over her social status.

"I go on a date with my boyfriend, get drunk, go home with his friend, and do it with him in my parents' house. Sounds pretty slutty to me."

"Do it?" I assumed she meant we had slept together, but I couldn't remember. I hesitated.

"Didn't we?"

"I don't recall." She looked a bit ashamed or perhaps hurt. I realized that if we had committed this sin, she would certainly hope that I would remember it, and if I insisted that we hadn't, she would wonder why I had not taken the liberty.

"If we had slept together, I would certainly remember doing so."

She nodded a hopeful agreement, signaling to me that I was following her emotional lead correctly.

"So we must not have slept together." We were both very pleased with my logic.

"Thank God. I assumed the worst."

"Of yourself?"

"Of you, of course," she clarified.

"Well, I am very sorry. I trust this will not improve your general opinion of men?"

She smiled a bit, so I continued.

"You may rest assured that my failure to take advantage of you may be attributed to excessive use of alcohol, rather than a noble character." I was piling it on, and I doubted she believed the bit regarding my noble character, but relief spread across her face and she brightened.

"You won't tell anyone, will you?"

"Tell them what? I think there's nothing to be ashamed of."

Her eyes widened with fear. Clearly this was not an episode of her life she wished to share with the world, especially the world packed into that ballroom. What she wanted was that our indiscretion, whatever it was, should magically disappear. And why shouldn't it? I had seen far greater improprieties boil away into nothing. Why not this one?

"Let us never speak of this again, to each other or anyone else."

"You mean it?"

"Sure. I would do almost anything to avoid incarceration. After all, you still have the legal advantage over me."

"You are wonderful," she said. She leaned forward, placed her delicate hands on my chest, lifted herself onto the tips of her toes, and pressed her perfect pink lips to mine. She lingered there just a moment, lips and hands against me. Then she performed a sublime release, lowering herself from her toes so that her lips gave the impression of being taken away rather than concluding the kiss. Her hands remained where they were.

"Thank you," she said, backing up slowly.

My head was swimming. I reached for her awkwardly and missed. She smiled, turned away, and walked into the haunted foliage, looking back at me only once before she disappeared. What a perfect kiss, a perfect girl, both coming and going. Milton could really pick them, I mused to myself and stared into the sky, burnt orange by the city lights.

Here on the golf course, at the intersection between New Orleans and Metairie, I took a moment to breathe in the heady vapors of dissonant culture and my dissonant life. Perhaps that dissonance was culture. Tennessee Williams said there were only three cities in the United States: New York, San Francisco, and New Orleans. Everywhere else is Cleveland. I had always thought Williams simply didn't like Cleveland, but then it struck me, standing on the golf course at the New Orleans Country Club. He wasn't talking about what was wrong with Cleveland but what was right about New Orleans, and what was right about it, what he loved about it, was that it was all wrong. These few American cities maintained disjointed elements of the old world, of Rome, Paris, London. Though we exalt the orderly rhythms of efficiency and standardization that define most of the American landscape, culture flourishes in the discord of antinomies. There on the golf course, I tried to embrace my own antinomies.

"How romantic," came a voice from the dark.

It was Jane.

27

BLINKED HARD AND RUBBED MY LIPS, hoping to wipe away the kiss. It didn't work. I turned to face her. My eyes were glazed, and my lips still burned of Holly. Jane was leaning casually against a tree, toying with a cigarette.

"Cute girl. Care for a cigarette?" She held out her hand, offering me the pack. "I'm giving them up."

I stuttered a few words and then stopped. I had been looking forward to speaking with Jane all day, presumably with the intention of clarifying my feelings for her or convincing her to reconsider her engagement plans. Although I still wasn't sure to what end that clarification or convincing was intended, I knew that it shouldn't begin with my kissing Holly.

She sensed my nervousness. "Relax, idiot. I'm not the kissing police. I won't tell her parents."

I recalled what Roberto had said and decided to go on the offensive. "I've been looking for you all evening." I sounded absurd.

"Did you believe I was in Holly's mouth?"

It didn't work.

"You know Holly?" I was surprised, forgetting that Jane and Holly had both been at brunch.

"It is her debutante party. Of course I know who she is, although I must say I was surprised not to see her in the receiving line when I came in. I should have known that you or Milton or any of his rakes would be responsible for her delinquency. Her mother told me she had gone to the powder room. Imagine that."

"Holly is Milton's girlfriend. We were just resolving a confusion."

"That you are not Milton? I can see why she might get confused. Middle-aged man who chases young girls—how is she to tell you two apart?"

Middle-aged? This tack wasn't working either. I had to try something more direct. I asked for a cigarette to stall for time. Jane happily obliged. Roberto, I must remember what Roberto had said. Talk about love, talk only about love. That is the only thing women really care about. I knew it was absurd advice, but it was all I had. Jane lit my cigarette. I took a deep, cancerous breath.

"I love you," I said, smoke dripping from my lips.

Jane dropped the lighter, bent down to look for it in the dark, and stood up immediately without having recovered it.

"What?" she asked in an annoyed voice.

The problem with saying "I love you" is that there isn't much you can say afterward. There is only the hope that the woman expresses the same emotion. Then you can take her in your arms and kiss her. On the other hand, she may mumble some nonsense about not feeling the same way, but in that case, it is she who must do the talking. Jane's reply placed the responsibility back on me, but what could I say? Repeat myself? I wasn't quite sure how I had gotten it out the first time and was not convinced I could do it again.

I decided to take the tough guy approach. I threw the cigarette on the ground, stepped on it, and said, "You heard me. I love you."

"You love me? Do you say that to all the girls you bring out here on the golf course? Is that how you get them to kiss you? I love you," she said in a sticky-sweet voice.

I tried to shut her up. "Yes, I love you."

"So? You love me. What am I supposed to do with that? Spit back some nonsense about loving you, so you can take me in your arms and kiss me? And then what, Tim?"

She looked me straight in the eye. Apparently, she was reading my mind. Or all men were the same, and she had met enough to figure us out. She was angry. Then she looked away. She started to say something. Both knees bent inward and her hands began moving as if she were speaking, but nothing was coming out. She was weakening. Was she waiting to be convinced? Perhaps, but I couldn't figure out what she wanted to be convinced of. Now I was stuck. Stuck here. Stuck with "I love you" and nothing more. What does a woman want? Roberto said they wanted love. I had given it to her. Now what was I to do? I was thinking too much, but I couldn't stop myself. I was thinking about what I had done and getting mad about it. I had just professed my love to my brother's fiancée and found it unrequited. Or had I? I wasn't sure, but my frustration kept building. I was suddenly mad at Jane, mad at Milton, and especially mad at Roberto. Idiot, never listen to an Italian talking about love. What do they know of love? Silly little language of theirs, everything sounds romantic. It doesn't matter what you say. But in English, you have to be clever. Perhaps I should have said it in Italian.

I shrugged my shoulders. "I don't know what else to say, Jane."

"Try something clever."

"I thought 'I love you' was clever."

"Not clever enough," she said, kneeling again to pick up the lighter. I had been right about Roberto. Asshole.

"I need a drink. Can I buy you one?" she asked.

"At the open bar?"

"I learned it from you, you cheap bastard," she said as she turned and walked back toward the party. But she kept talking. "All those damn dates we went on in college, you never paid."

I was still five paces behind her. "We were just friends."

The sound of metal grinding against metal, followed by Wagner's "Ride of the Valkyries," interrupted my defense. I caught up with Jane, who was almost back at the building. With a clear view of the club's parking lot, we watched as a confused valet stepped out of a beige K-car, a blue-green light reflecting off the front windshield and Wagner pouring from the driver's open door. The nose of the car was pressed tightly against the rear of a black, four-door BMW.

"I think that's William's car," Jane mentioned, almost in passing.

"The K-car on its way to Valhalla?" Of course I knew it wasn't.

"The BMW," she said, annoyed, knowing I was teasing her.

As I readily knew, Milton's heads-up display took some getting used to. Hoping to avoid any further distractions from an already messy evening, and not caring much about Milton's K-car or William's BMW, I took Jane by the arm and escorted her away from the accident. We entered the ballroom through the main entrance and were marshaled toward the receiving line. The flow of taffeta and tuxedo traffic in that direction was still steady, as many of the early guests who had skipped the formality for the bar were now returning to receive their official welcome from their hosts. Ahead of us were Milton, Roberto, and the Arizona brothers, each complimenting one another on their dashing attire.

"I have already been through. I believe I will go get that drink," Jane announced.

I started to join her, when I heard Milton's booming voice pierce the general din of the party.

THE ENGAGEMENT

Women hate revolutions and revolutionists.
They like men who are docile, and well
regarded at the bank, and never late at meals.

H. L. Mencken

CHAMPAGNE COCKTAIL

3 OZ CHAMPAGNE
½ OZ COGNAC
1 DASH ANGOSTURA BITTERS
1 SUGAR CUBE

Add a lemon twist, orange
twist, or slice of peach.

28

"TIMOTHY SCHMIDT! GODDAMN, you look well this evening!"

Milton pushed his heavy body toward me, shook my hand hard with one hand of his, while wrapping his other around my shoulders in an awkward hug.

"Please, introduce me to your friends," emphasizing the "your" and pointing at Roberto and the Arizona brothers. At first, I figured Milton presumed that if his gang was introduced as my guests, they were more likely to be welcomed. On second thought, however, I realized that he did not trust the brothers to understand the finer points of debutante etiquette and wanted to inure his standing in New Orleans society from any faux pas on their part. Obviously, he wasn't concerned with my reputation. I played along, although I suspected there was something more to his behavior.

Fortunately for both of us, his revolutionary gang had never looked better. Against the background of the other gentlemen's black attire, the Arizona brothers shone like stars in their matching white tuxedos. Their initial apprehension in their rented suits was now replaced by pride in their bold fashion statement. Roberto wore a sleek black jacket over a cream-colored shirt, tucked into black, close-fitted slacks. A tie that matched the shirt completed his fine getup and transformed him into a Mediterranean prince.

Above all, Milton carved a noble figure, coursing the room in his vintage coattails over a matching vest and capacious trousers, the whole ensemble finished with a broad bow tie that exploded across his chest and gave him the appearance of a grand toreador. He gesticulated madly as he spoke, causing his coat to twirl like a *muleta* and making his massive aspect appear to double in size. He filled the entire foyer with his dramatic geometry, observing as well as conducting all movements in this first *tercio*.

Milton pushed me closer to Roberto and the Arizona brothers and began shaking their hands. He did this directly in front of my mother, who was preparing to give each of them her official welcome.

"This is Roberto Palmieri, the famous Italian actor from Milan," I said to Milton so that others could hear. And then to my mother, "And these two gentlemen are old college friends who are visiting from Arizona."

My mother gave me a puzzled, disappointed look. It was certainly not proper form for me to drag two old drinking buddies to my sister's debut. I looked her in the eye and knew I must do better by her and my family.

"They are in town on business. They represent a West Coast banking magnate in a possible merger with Hibernia Bank." I was no expert on etiquette, so I couldn't be sure this would legitimize their appearance at the party, but my mother had always hoped Tabatha would marry money, and I figured that the possibility of them being wealthy bankers would gloss over any breach of debutante decorum their presence might occasion.

"Mrs. Schmidt," each brother said in turn, taking my mother's hand.

My mother ignored that I had not mentioned their names and simply answered with, "Gentlemen, allow me to introduce to you my daughter, Ms. Tabatha Michelle Schmidt."

My banker ploy had worked. They moved along the line, my sister then introducing them to the Trenchards as Arizona bankers and so on to Mrs. Calloway and some other Calloway women. Holly and Mr. Calloway were absent, which was a relief to me.

Roberto took my mother's hand, lifted it, and gave it a long, moist kiss.

"*Buona sera,*" he said. "Roberto Palmieri."

My mother was a bit taken aback by the kiss, but she remembered Roberto's previous service and told him it was always a pleasure to have him in her company. Milton stepped in quickly and distracted her, probably fearful that a longer conversation may reveal unnecessary details about Roberto's true occupation, which was a complete mystery to me. Roberto continued the kisses all the way down the receiving line. This played well with the debutantes, who delighted in his accent, which they probably thought lent the party a cosmopolitan flavor.

In greeting my mother, Milton bowed deeply, so deeply that when he swept his hand forward it nearly hit the ground. This was no small accomplishment for a man of Milton's size. The gesture pleased my mother, who praised Milton's fine upbringing, although at that angle Milton's tremendous backside may have appeared somewhat obscene to the ladies and gentlemen standing behind him. He bowed again to my sister, and not wishing to be outdone by Roberto, took her hand and kissed it through the duration of the bow. Tabatha beamed with pride and greeted him in a voice that seemed to welcome him to more than just the party. I was offended. Milton lingered with Tabatha; she flirted shamelessly.

I stepped up and introduced myself. "Good evening, miss, and thank you for having me."

Tabatha growled at me, but Milton chose to avoid a scene. He offered her hand a final kiss and then moved on to the next in line.

"Disgraceful," I said to Tabatha. She growled again before offering the gentleman behind me a warm welcome. This move effectively completed our encounter. Seeing that neither Holly nor her father was present, I bounced through the remainder in a wholly forgettable fashion, which was not difficult to do considering the commotion that Milton and his legion were creating: each bowing and kissing.

Holly's absence was not conspicuous. The debutantes were not expected to man the line like Spartans, but it certainly made Milton's overtures to my sister easier. How Milton planned to negotiate this new double-date dilemma was not, for a change, my problem.

Jane was gone. From where I stood just inside the main ballroom, I couldn't see her. The room was now full of partygoers, and it would have been easy for her to disappear or to hide from me, if that is what she wished. After the episode on the golf course, I was sure she had run back to William. That had been my chance. I had had her alone in a romantic spot. Kissing Holly had really blown it. There was nowhere to go from there. It was done. I could already imagine William surrounded in the center of the ballroom, mouth open in an operatic yawn, announcing his engagement to Jane.

Milton snatched me as I emerged from the end of the line. "Thanks for helping us through. You were marvelous."

His gang encircled me and offered me nods and slaps of appreciation.

"I suppose I should be grateful that the Anglo-German contingent isn't here."

"Not yet," said Milton, "but I did mention it to Stefan last night. He and Andrew may yet make an appearance."

"Lovely."

"Let me buy you a Scotch," the black brother said buoyantly. "Are you serving Scotch?" he added hopefully.

"You're the third person to offer to buy me a drink this evening. Everyone is feeling universally generous, knowing that my inheritance is paying the bill."

Milton smiled and put his massive, tuxedoed arm around me.

"Dear boy, when my revolution is complete, your inheritance will be worthless. You may as well enjoy its liquidation this evening." He chuckled at his own cleverness, paused, and then chuckled some more. "By the way, I saw you talking to Jane. How are things going?"

"Not well," I admitted.

"Why did she bugger off?" asked Milton.

They all looked at me carefully.

"Did you say something?" the white brother inquired.

"I told her I loved her."

"Ha!" shouted Milton.

"Bravo," Roberto said, giving me a stiff whack across the back.

"Well done, well done," said the black brother.

"Perhaps, but she wasn't nearly so impressed as y'all."

"That is because women are idiots," cried Milton. "If only they were more like men. In fact, it is a pity we poor bastards must seduce women at all. Seduction would be a far more handsome thing if women were men."

"Totally," said the white brother. "If I were a chick, I would have bought it."

"Wait a minute," warned Milton. He held up his hands to silence everyone and then cast a suspicious glance my way. "How did you say it?" He pretended to address me but actually delivered the question to the brothers and Roberto.

"I just said it."

"Where?"

"I think we were on the golf course."

Approving nods emerged all around, followed by confusion.

"You had her on the golf course, you told her you love her, I don't get it? What could be wrong here?"

"She did catch me kissing another woman."

Everyone looked up, except Roberto. Perhaps he didn't understand.

"Another woman?" Milton asked in disbelief.

"Dude, this place must rock," asserted the black brother.

"Who?" asked Milton.

"If you must know, it was Holly."

Everyone froze, and then they all spoke at once.

"Jesus H. Christ."

"Holly?"

"Wasn't that the chick Milton was with last night?"

"Dude, what does the 'H' stand for?"

The questions came in a flurry. I made no effort to answer them. I merely shrugged, nodded, and said yes. What was I to say?

"Bad timing dude."

"Sucks to be you."

"You did steal my girlfriend," Milton added in feigned horror. "I knew it, you backstabbing, girlfriend-stealing—"

"Easy there, big guy," I interrupted and discovered a new courage that was probably gin-induced. "If you recall, it was you who set me up on a date with her."

"Did you sleep with her?" Milton asked as casually as if he were asking for the sports section of the newspaper.

At this moment, Roberto looked up and said, "No, this is not the issue. This kissing the other woman is of no importance."

"What?" asked one of the brothers.

"Dude?" asked the other.

It was a fortunate interruption, as I did not care to explain that while I had slept with Holly, I had probably not had sex with her, and could not say anything without breaking my promise to Holly. Milton seemed content to allow the subject to die. Perhaps because he was finished with Holly. Perhaps because he really meant it when he said he didn't treat women like property. But, most likely, because there are some things friends can never discuss cordially.

"The woman does not care about the other woman," insisted Roberto. "She cares only about herself. This other woman is not your problem."

I didn't trust him at all. But he spoke with such cool authority, we were all left listening to him.

"Your problem lies elsewhere. What did she say when you told her you love her?"

"I don't know," I lied.

"Think man, think," demanded Milton, "this is important."

"She asked me what she was supposed to do about it."

Everyone stood still, looking at me. Roberto ran his hand across his chin.

"Ah, this Jane is a very clever woman. Wine!" he commanded. "We must have wine."

Without any reply, we all turned and moved toward the adjacent ballroom, aiming for the bar where my father and I had begun the evening. The main hall was full now, with most of the guests mingling around the swan and hors d'oeuvres, absorbed in small talk. Only the elderly sat. Weaving through the buzzing mass, I kept my eye out for William and Jane. Nothing. The crowd was too dense, or Jane was hiding too well. My search was further hindered by constant interruptions from family friends, greeting me to ask how I was, how long I had been in town, what I was doing, whom I had seen. I couldn't keep up with the others, and in their lust for drink, I was abandoned in a sea of New Orleans bourgeoisie. The band began playing what sounded like a top-twenty tune, but I didn't recognize it. Apparently, nobody else did either, because no one was dancing except the busty, blonde singer, who was obviously chosen for her physical assets rather than her musical ones.

When I finally made it to the bar, I discovered that my father and his drinking companion had been replaced by two young girls with whom Milton and Roberto had obviously had some previous acquaintance. Both wore short cocktail dresses: one forest green, the other a shiny mauve, if mauve could ever be considered shiny. I heard Milton mention how lovely they both looked before he asked if he could buy them a drink. The bartender immediately produced two glasses of red wine, which the girls accepted with giggles and thank yous. The brothers were relishing plates stacked high with food they must have procured along the trek and were discussing the marvelous ice swan that had provided sustenance for them like the swan on the Louisiana flag. I did not have the heart to tell them that the beast on the flag was a pelican, rending its own flesh to feed its offspring, yet somehow this metaphor seemed appropriate to the occasion. New Orleans' bourgeois society was not only wining and dining Milton's gang, they were offering up their flesh and blood in the form of their daughters to this next generation of Marxists intent on overthrowing the capitalism that made bourgeois society possible.

"I don't believe I have seen you since Mardi Gras last year," Roberto said to the girl in green, taking her hand as he did. She surrendered fully to his charms and pressed herself against him in a way I am sure would horrify her mother.

Milton too was making significant headway with the shiny girl in mauve. She had already tucked her arm under his and laughed, as if on cue, at each of his pithy comments.

"I have acquired a marvelous automobile since we last met. Perhaps you would care to take a drive with me this evening?"

It was clear that everything he said to this girl had been rehearsed, designed to prevent his sounding average. I couldn't resist interrupting him, hoping to throw him off his game.

"Magnificent, indeed, though significantly less magnificent this evening than it was this afternoon."

Milton's girl gave me a disapproving look. Apparently, his charm trumped his ownership of an automobile, and this young lass was trying very hard to make that clear, but the comment intrigued Milton, whose curiosity exceeded even the most feral cat. So the game began. He looked at me and paused. He sensed a trap but was far too proud to refuse the challenge. I could tell he was calculating the best way to ask me what I was talking about, without sounding average. So long as he could maintain his composure, he would win. But should he falter, show distress, I would prevail.

He opened his mouth slowly, forming the words meticulously. "Has some ill befallen my motorcar?" It was not Shakespeare, but it worked for his girl.

Now it was my turn, but I was already prepared.

"That depends upon your taste in hood ornaments. In this case, I believe it was a BMW."

Milton knew he had been set up. He choked back a laugh and gave me a nod to acknowledge my rhetorical triumph. But he wasn't fully defeated. He took a moment to compose himself and calmly replied, "While I have never been impressed with the Bavarian Motor Works aesthetic, I understand that they are very fashionable these days amongst the lower middle class. May I ask who was responsible for this accessorizing in my absence?"

"I think it was the valet. He seemed unsettled by your movie selection."

Milton took a long breath. He relaxed and gave in. Perhaps he could have gone on, but not for the sake of this girl. "Is there anything left?"

I too relented, now that victory was mine. "I think it will get you home, though the BMW may not have been as fortunate."

Milton laughed and turned to his girl. "Well, it seems that our drive may require a rain check. But if we are not going to be driving, we might as well be drinking. More wine!" he said to the bartender, who was quick with the bottle.

"To fast cars!" toasted Milton.

"To fast women!" toasted a brother.

"To my brother's BMW!" I added, with a smirk that quickly spread from my face to Milton's and signaled my return to a kinder, simpler life, where what a person said, and how one said it, still mattered.

"To *amore!*" said Roberto, giving his girl a squeeze and a delicate kiss. He then turned to me and put a hand on my shoulder. "She doesn't trust you."

"What?" I said, looking at Roberto and his green girl with suspicion.

"I don't know, but she doesn't trust you. She doesn't think you mean it. You must show her you do."

"Who?"

"Milton," Roberto said, poking him, "I forget her name. That plain girl he likes. What is she called?"

"Jane," Milton said flatly.

"Yes, of course, Jane."

I was a bit miffed at their conducting this lesson in front of the two young ladies, but I made no effort to stop them. My moment of rhetorical triumph had passed, and I was returned to the harsh reality of my romantic failure.

"Grab her and kiss her, dude," asserted one of the brothers.

"Totally," added the other.

Milton just nodded and drained his wine.

"Allow me to show you how it's done," said the white brother.

"He can't show you crap. He doesn't know shit about women. I'll show you," the black brother bragged, and both stormed off, presumably on the prowl for women upon whom they might demonstrate their artistry.

"This should be amusing," I said to Milton and his mauve maiden.

Milton shrugged, welcomed another glass of wine, and leaned against the bar. "Roberto is right. Sincerity

is the key to proclamations of love. An insincere proc-
lamation will do more damage than if you knock her on
the ground and grope her."

"Are you recommending that I knock her down?"

"No, I am recommending that you display some
sincerity."

"I was sincere."

"You miss my point. I don't care if you are sincere or
not. I don't care how you feel. What matters is that you
behave in such a manner as to portray sincerity."

"Let me get this straight," I was both amused and
annoyed now. "It's not important that I am sincere, but
only that I appear to be sincere?"

"Fair enough," said Milton. Roberto nodded in agreement. The two girls nodded as well.

"And my sincere sincerity is not sincere enough?" I
asked.

"Apparently not," Milton said, shrugging his shoulders. Roberto nodded again, accepting a glass of wine
from the bartender.

"So what do I do? Fake a sincere declaration of my
feelings?"

Roberto shrugged his shoulders this time, and Milton
nodded and agreed. "Works for me. It will probably
work for you."

I was suddenly exhausted.

"Look, women are just like us. They don't have any
mystical capacity to see your heart or read your mind.
They don't know what you really think. All they can do is
judge your actions. What we men ask as evidence of love
is that she sleep with us. Girl sleeps with you, you know

she digs you. Simple enough. But women know that most men sleep with women rather indiscriminately."

Changing his tone, Milton continued, "I should mention that this tendency has done more damage to the art of seduction than any other single factor."

Roberto nodded, but it was not clear that he was following the conversation. He kept looking out across the ballroom to keep an eye on the brothers.

"Women can't judge your affections with sex. This puts them at a great disadvantage, and they feel it. To make Jane believe you love her, you have to do something, something grand."

"And what counts as grand? Not your bowing and kissing, I hope."

"Well, I am certainly doing better with your sister than you are with Jane. But there are plenty of methods available to you. In some parts of this state, folks paint their affections on interstate overpasses."

The girl in the mauve dress pulled away from Milton and asked, "Who is his sister?"

Milton ignored her.

I glared at him.

"Expensive jewelry usually works."

Roberto's girl nodded.

Roberto added, "Expensive anything," and finished his wine.

"Why do you think rich guys get beautiful women? Sure, they like the money, but it's more than just money. When a guy spends a lot on a woman, the woman feels special. And that is all women really want—to feel special."

"I haven't any jewelry. But the I-10 overpass does run directly in front of the club. Shall I scale the supports with a can of spray paint?"

"Not a bad idea," Milton ignored my disdain. "The trick is that it must be big with no reservations. Despite her mouth, Jane is a classy girl, and the overpass gambit may not find its full effect with her. You need something assertive, while still sophisticated. That's why your brother nailed her."

I sneered at him.

"Sorry, just an expression. But you've got to give William credit. He may be a graceless barbarian, but he is decisive. Decisive will always win the day."

"Declare your love for her in front of everyone here," suggested Roberto.

"Yeah," added Milton, raising his glass.

"Perfect. I declare my love for her in front of my brother. That will go over well."

But my jest lost its punch to a punch thrown by a brother. Roberto's eyes widened and a whispered "Madonna" slipped from his lips. Milton and I looked up from our conversation but did not enjoy Roberto's line of sight into the adjacent ballroom. I stood up on the top rungs of the barstool so to discover the source of Roberto's concern. What I saw should have shocked me. The Arizona brothers were facing off in front of the Swan-protected hors d'oeuvres. They were surrounded by young, smiling girls. The band stopped, and I could now both see and hear the proceedings.

"You have insulted this fair lady's honor, dude," shouted the black brother over the general party din.

"Honor?" The white brother lifted a large glass, half full of red wine. I could only imagine the other half was inspiring his bravado. "I will fight to the death," he paused for a drink, "to defend her honor." He lifted the glass again, this time higher, as if in a toast.

In response, the black brother raised his own wineglass, though this one full, shouted something incomprehensible, and then drank.

I was not typically cool under pressure, but I felt none of the astonishment that should have accompanied the demise of my sister's debut.

"Should we do something?" I asked.

"It's probably too late," said Milton. "Once they have gotten this far, you can't stop them. You can only hope to contain them."

The men in the vicinity steadily backed away from the brothers. Two rescued their drinks from a table before fleeing the scene. The women remained, and others moved in to determine the cause. I could see my mother, Aunt Dee, Tabatha, and Sarah approaching the ruckus. Mrs. Calloway was signaling her husband to do something. He chose to ignore her and the entire incident. Perhaps he was still wearing his reading glasses, or perhaps he had already endured as many incidents as his constitution could bear in one day.

"What is going on?" asked Roberto's girl.

"Nothing we cannot manage," answered Milton, "but you should find your parents and recommend that they stand clear."

Both girls obeyed him immediately, disappearing into the crowd.

"Are there likely to be police?" asked Roberto. "I cannot afford to be arrested, as my visa has expired."

"Yes, friend, keep back," Milton said, "I wouldn't want you compromised. You are far too important to the cause." To the bartender, he added, "Another round of wine, sir, and a small bottle of soda water."

"What cause is that?" asked Roberto.

"His binging and debauchery, I suppose," I replied quietly.

Milton gave me a hurt look. The wine came in fresh glasses, and Milton raised a toast to the evening and his revolution.

"You see, disbeliever, this ballroom represents the moneyed society of our nation. Now you will see that society cast into anarchy. This is the cause," he said softly. "Do you not see my hand in it?" he looked at me and smiled. "To the cause!"

We all drank, Roberto and I not completely sure what we were drinking to, but happy enough to drink. Milton dropped the bottle of soda water into his jacket pocket and gestured to me to follow him, with a nod to Roberto and then, "Hussars, to battle!"

We hustled toward the center of the ballroom, where the brothers were surrounded by layers of bewildered partygoers. This was clearly uncharted territory for the upper crust of New Orleans society. They watched, expressing something between fear and indignation at the scene now unfolding. Was this really happening? Were the Arizona brothers about to brawl among the debutantes and devotees? It seemed surreal.

"Did you stage this?" I asked Milton in an accusative tone.

"Only providence can stage such a magnificent happening as this. Trust in it alone. It's amazing the direction our lives take when we submit to the cultural narrative. Come!"

This was said with perfect sincerity. I knew he was full of crap, but at the same time, I couldn't resist his call.

"This way," Milton said, taking my arm now and leading me through the oscillating crowd: men moving out, women flowing in.

I saw William on the opposite edge of the ballroom, working his way toward the action with two black waiters in tow. He was wearing a broad-fitting, double-breasted tuxedo and walking as if with a purpose, shoving people aside, making way for the three of them. The waiters seemed apprehensive but stayed in step with William. He broke through the final ring of women and entered the circle just as we reached my mother, Aunt Dee, and Tabatha. The crowd on our side was rather tight, because most of the space was occupied by the table supporting the splendid ice swan. Unwilling to upset the table in an effort to squeeze through and unwilling to push the ladies aside, Milton and I were relegated to watching from behind them.

"Oh heavens," started my mother. "What is William up to?"

"Oh, I hope there won't be a scene," added Aunt Dee.

The brothers began to circle. William shouted something at one of the waiters and pointed toward the white brother. Reluctantly, the waiter moved up and grabbed him by the arm.

"Oh no," whispered Milton. I knew this meant trouble. Milton was not the sort to fret over nothing. The white brother shouted a guttural yelp, whirled, twisted, and fell to the ground.

"Barbarian!" shouted the black brother, rushing to his brother's rescue. Drunken arms flailing, the black brother smacked the surprised waiter in the head with his wineglass, sending wine and glass cascading across the ballroom. Tabatha leaned forward to glimpse the action at the wrong moment and became a victim of the airborne libation.

"Oh heavens," my mother repeated. "That will stain."

With catlike precision, Milton snatched a napkin from the table, drew the bottle of soda water from his jacket pocket, opened the top, and said to my mother, "Allow me, ma'am." He displayed the soda water and then knelt down on one knee, beginning to dab Tabatha's dress with the moistened cloth.

Inside the circle, the waiter fell to the floor, as much from surprise as the blow to the head. William jumped upon the black brother, grabbing both of his arms. In their struggle, they stumbled over the supine white brother and landed in a mass against the parquet.

"What a gentleman!" my mother proclaimed, admiring Milton's handiwork with the soda. "There are so few men who can handle an emergency these days."

The white brother turned over and grabbed the bludgeoned waiter by the leg, dragging him back to the ground just as he had gained his feet. The second waiter appeared, set on joining in but was unclear as to how to proceed. William and the black brother rolled toward us and the swan. Fists were flying; none was landing. A general gasp rose above the clamor, as the guests anticipated the demise of both the bird and the still plentiful hors d'oeuvres.

Milton worked on the dress diligently, ignoring the brawl before him. My mother, aunts, and Tabatha had also forgotten the fight and were focused on the dress.

Apparently, one of the other mothers couldn't bear to see the table upset. Exercising questionable judgment, she stepped between the rolling mass of William and the black brother. She pointed an accusing finger but was quickly knocked over. Backward she fell, across the oysters, shrimp, crabs, crawfish, artichokes, carrots, and broccoli, scattering seafood, sauces, and vegetable crudités onto the nearest onlookers. Her momentum was halted by the swan, which absorbed the impact—but for all its size and apparent weight still slid quite effortlessly along the table and dove gracelessly off the side. It shattered easily, adding to the general chaos, which now included shouting, screaming, cursing, pushing. The band was still not playing, but the busty, blonde singer could be heard shrieking in astonishment. The brothers kept fighting.

I heard a German voice in the crowd.

"What happened to the music?"

I craned my neck to see if it was Stefan with his French Quarter contingent, and while scanning the pandemonium, Jane appeared next to me.

She looked lovely. How had I not noticed it before? A splendid long black dress, her hair pulled back in a comb, a thin strand running delicately along each side of her face. In her hand was a champagne flute, the champagne untouched. She appeared utterly unfazed by the action, but she had a very serious look about her.

"Timothy," she said in a stern voice, "you must do something."

At first, I wasn't sure what she meant. Her arrival had completely thrown me off guard, and I temporarily forgot the turmoil that had engulfed the party. Could she mean do something about us? About her? But what? Why now? Her face betrayed that she was not thinking of herself.

"Have you forgotten the guests and the young girls for whom the evening has been fashioned?"

I hated that she was so considerate of others. It made me feel guilty for being so self-absorbed. I hated feeling guilty.

"Why me?" was all I could think to ask. But it was a stupid question.

I turned from her and pressed through the crowd toward the bandstand. The musicians gazed lifelessly at the ruckus in total confusion. I begged the busty, blonde singer to borrow her microphone.

Grasping it by the cord, she held it out to me like a flaccid, useless thing and in a squeaky, subdued voice said, "Here." From the stage, I enjoyed a perfect panorama of the mayhem. In front of me, the crowd had engulfed the combatants. In the adjacent ballroom, Roberto was back at the bar, sipping wine with his arm slung comfortably around Holly. She was sitting contentedly, legs crossed, head back, glass of red wine in her hand—a casual observer to the demise of her own debut. Roberto was obviously a master of his trade. At the entrance, two police officers were pushing their way into the building. And there, in the center of it all, was Jane, standing alone, staring at me as if saying, "What are you going to do about this?"

I wasn't sure, so I lifted the microphone to my mouth and announced, "May I have your attention!"

The volume must have been near its limit, perhaps to compensate for the blonde's delicate voice. My amplified words knocked half the crowd down, but it created the desired effect. Everyone stopped in mid-action and looked at me. The police stopped advancing. Milton stopped dabbing. Roberto turned his attention from Holly. The Arizona brothers stopped fighting. There was a moment of quiet, and I knew I must seize it. I held out my hand in Jane's direction and motioned for her to come to me. She responded with a doubtful look but started navigating a path.

Seize the moment, seize the moment, I thought.

"It is my distinct pleasure to inform you that Jane, uh," I hesitated, still not sure what I would do. My eyes met Milton's. He had a curious grin on his face. Then I saw Roberto. He was nodding his head. I was still unsure. Then my brother stood up, disheveled from his battle with Milton's brothers.

"What the hell is going on?" he said, loud enough to draw the eyes of the crowd. The bastard. He was preparing to assert his will. I could see it in his eyes. It was a strong will. I had rarely resisted it. I had failed to resist him at The Columns Hotel and failed to resist him at Commander's Palace. I felt my hands begin to quiver and my palms moisten on the microphone. I was nervous. Was I really going to let him take over this party the way he had the brunch?

Jane was in front of me now, and as our eyes met, I felt a need for courage. This is not quite the same thing as courage. I am not sure I had ever felt courage. Courage is facing up to your fears and overcoming them. Nothing in me seemed prepared to overcome anything, but I knew that if I let William win, I would feel guilty. And I hated feeling guilty. I reached out, took Jane by the hand, and pulled her onto the low stage next to me.

"Family and friends, it is my pleasure to announce to you that Jane Tomlinson and I are engaged to be married."

I could see William's mouth open, a bit of blood splashed across his lips, but his words, if there were any, were drowned out by the general expressions of congratulations and perfunctory clapping. My mother looked directly at me, but I couldn't read her expression: pleasure or pain? It was unclear. Roberto was shouting "Bravo!" from his seat at the bar.

Milton raised his small bottle of soda water and exclaimed in a penetrating voice, "A toast to Timothy and Jane!"

Ever the romantic, he turned to Tabatha, "And to our wonderful and beautiful hostesses this evening."

From the looks my mother and sister beamed back at him, I knew his seduction had succeeded again. What a simple thing it was, really. I suppose that was his genius: the distillation of simplicity and clarity from complexity and chaos.

Glasses were raised all around. A passing waiter offered me champagne. Roberto refreshed his wine.

I turned to Jane, not sure if I was prepared for her reaction to the announcement. She was smiling and holding my hand. Not the elated grin of unbridled enthusiasm I was hoping to see. Perhaps it was relief she wore on her face. I lifted my glass to her, and she touched it gently with her own. We drank to loud applause. I looked out over the crowd at William. His eyes were set, aimed directly at me. What would he do? I looked back at Jane.

Reading my mind, she said, "Relax, he'll do nothing now. There are too many people."

"He may still kill me," I added.

"Perhaps." She looked at him and noticed the blank flush of fury on his face. "Or perhaps we should leave," she said, "now that you've rescued your sister's party."

I nodded in agreement. I handed the empty champagne flutes to the blonde and led Jane toward the front entrance. We received many congratulations all the way to the door.

"Did you drive?" she asked.

"No, did you?"

"No, but I have William's keys."

"Excellent."

We returned to the parking lot and the site of the accident.

The valet had moved the K-car slightly backward, so that the front bumper was no longer inside the BMW's wheel well. The K-car looked like hell, but it had always looked that way. William's BMW looked worse. The front end on the driver's side was caved in. It wasn't going anywhere anytime soon. Jane looked at me.

"Milton's car?"

Jane shrugged assent.

I opened the driver's side door for her, and she slid across the front seat to the other side. I then settled in behind the customized command center of Milton's K-car.

"Timothy!" I heard a shout from the shadows. It was my brother. I didn't know what to expect. Perhaps, like Jane, he was relieved. Perhaps he was relieved of the pressure of doing the honorable thing.

"You bastard!" he yelled across the parking lot. I guess he wasn't relieved.

"Do you have the key?" Jane asked.

"Don't need one," I quipped. I turned the ignition. The engine sputtered, the windshield filled with helicopters killing people on a beach, Wagner's "Ride of the Valkyries" blasted from the rear speakers, and that curious gasoline smell rose up from somewhere beneath. I threw the car in gear and took off.

"Where are we going?" Jane asked over the trumpets and trombones.

"I don't know. I can't see through the movie. It looks like Vietnam."

Milton had chosen *Apocalypse Now* to set the tone for his gang's arrival at the debutante affair. Now it was setting the tone for my engagement. I avoided a black Cadillac, two attack helicopters, and an exploding bamboo hut, turned right at the light, and ascended the interstate on-ramp. Driving through war-torn Vietnam was proving quite a challenge and failing to produce the romantic getaway I had envisioned. And now I was beginning to wonder what this all meant to Jane. Were we really engaged? I hoped so. I had announced it in front of hundreds of people. Surely she couldn't go back to William now. What had I actually done? Had I done anything at all? Or were we back on another date, with all the questions unanswered? Where was that damn toggle switch for the display? The anxiety of it all was overwhelming me.

I merged blindly onto the interstate and immediately turned my attention to Jane. Watching where I was going was made less important by the fact that I could only see aerial combat on the windshield.

"No, I mean, to where are we going?" she clarified. "What's our destination?"

"Oh, I don't know. Do you have a preference?" I had no idea what I was doing. I was having a hard enough time navigating New Orleans and Vietnam.

She said nothing, but out of the corner of my eye I could see her shrug, like Atlas, trying to dislodge the weight of the world.

"Boston?" She phrased the comment in such a way as to allow it to be as much a question as an answer.

"Why Boston?"

"To get away?" she said or asked, I wasn't sure.

"You can't get away. There is no away. It feels different when you go someplace else, but that's just an illusion. It's all New Orleans." I sounded dreadfully serious. "Anyway, Milton's revolution is going to make my occupation in Boston obsolete." Jane forced a laugh and looked out the passenger-side window.

"Your family throws quite a party," she said absent-mindedly.

"When was the last time you attended a debutante party that broke into a fight and was broken up by the police?" I said, still shocked by the conclusion of the ball.

"I have always thought debutante parties very dangerous. That is what gives them life, the bumping and scraping." She laughed and turned to look at me. She still seemed unsettled, which was only natural, given the circumstances.

"Do you want to go to Boston?" I ventured.

"No, thank you. I don't imagine this car would make it that far." She found the bottle of Paisano, just as two surfers were nearly blown to pieces on the windshield. She opened the top, smelled it, and winced.

"It's Paisano," I said, "a light Chianti."

"Hardly."

"It has the same name."

"This is America. Names are cheap. Wine is cheap. Everything is cheap," she said bitterly, rolling down her window and pouring the Paisano out. "What can we do?"

"Go to The Columns?" I asked.

"For Sazeracs?" she sounded skeptical.

"Sure." Seemed as good a plan as any. Certainly better than going to Boston. I always preferred a cocktail at The Columns to Boston.

"Not for me. I'm pregnant, remember?" She was speaking very deliberately and loudly, so as to be heard over the movie and the music. "I'll watch you and enjoy the ambiance."

"I'm not sure I'm in the mood to drink with an audience."

"Since when have you ever said no to a drink?"

"Only since I have been engaged."

"I hope you don't plan to make it a habit."

"Of being engaged?"

She laughed at me. Then she stopped and looked at me, with a twisted smile across her face. "You aren't the marrying type, Timothy."

"What do you mean?"

"You have now been engaged twice, and you still are not married. A girl would be silly to think engagements meant very much to you."

"This is only the second time."

"How often do you intend to do it?"

I wanted to answer, explain myself, but nothing came, well, nothing clever. At this point, I should have been accustomed to finding myself confronted with nothing, but I don't suppose a person ever becomes comfortable with it. A gloom threatened to come over me, and then, out of the darkness, something appeared.

"What does it mean?" I asked.

"What?"

"All of this. Everything that's happened."

"Us?"

"Sure."

"That life is like literature. It should never be taken seriously."

"What about you?" I asked. "Should I take you seriously?" I was suddenly worried.

"God no. You should never take a woman seriously. I hoped Milton might have at least taught you that."

The gloom threatened again, and then Jane reached over and took my hand, kissing it twice before placing it on her stomach. A broad smile crossed her face.

"The baby?" I asked.

"Yeah," she said.

"At least he will look like me."

"We'll see."

"What?" I asked, startled at her unsaid suggestion. I wavered in emotional ambivalence.

"Don't take it too seriously."

I withdrew my hand.

Jane struck the toggle switch and turned off the movie.

I stared at her for a moment and then at the windshield with its heads-up display, indicating our speed, fuel level, oil pressure. I started to speak. I stopped, started again, and stopped again. How did she know how to operate it? I stared at her some more.

She gave me a knowing smile.

I relaxed. I didn't understand. It was a muddled affair, and this was New Orleans. Nothing was going to make any sense here. There was no sense in trying to sort it out.

"One Sazerac at The Columns," I said.

She reached for my hand again, grasping it tightly.

I felt emboldened by her gesture. "Or perhaps a champagne cocktail. Surely you can allow yourself a glass of champagne to celebrate our engagement."

"And how long will it last?"

"That, my love, depends on how quickly you drink it."

JACK SIMMONS was born in California. He attended Mandeville High School in Louisiana as well as Louisiana State University and Tulane University.

He lives in Savannah, Georgia, with his wife Katherine and is the proud father of Savannah, Mary, and Augustus.

Although he is a professor of philosophy, he still finds time to enjoy a Sazerac cocktail in the evenings.

monte ceceri

SwanHorse Press is an imprint of
Monte Ceceri Publishers, LLC